Kevin Threlfall was born in Wolverhampton and educated at Denstone College near Uttoxeter. He was co-founder of Lo-Cost Discount Stores and founder of T&S Stores PLC, an operator of a countrywide chain of convenience stores.

After selling out to Tesco in 2003, he became a director of Wolverhampton Wanderers Football Club.

His interests include playing golf and watching most sports, travel and writing.

In 2014, he published his autobiography entitled: *One Stop One Life.*

This book is dedicated to my late father who inspired me with a love of cricket.

Kevin Threlfall

Stumped

AUSTIN MACAULEY PUBLISHERS™

LONDON • CAMBRIDGE • NEW YORK • SHARJAH

A CIP catalogue record for this title is available from the British Library.

ISBN 9781398462274 (Paperback)
ISBN 9781398462281 (Hardback)
ISBN 9781398462304 (ePub e-book)
ISBN 9781398462298 (Audiobook)

www.austinmacauley.com

First Published 2022
Austin Macauley Publishers Ltd®
1 Canada Square
Canary Wharf
London
E14 5AA

Chapter One

Jack Reed should have been born with a cricket bat in his hand because from the moment he could stand on his own two feet, he was never happier than when he was whacking a ball around the garden.

Cricket was well and truly in his blood as his father had been captain of the local village side for a number of years, and from the time he could peep over the sides of his pram, he was used to seeing people dressed in white clothes rushing around a lush green outfield.

The weekends were all about being down at the ground with mother making the teas, his elder sister doing the scoring and Dad charging in to bowl from the pavilion end. As Jack grew in stature and in age, it was inevitable that cricket would become a major part of his life.

And indeed, so it was, as he became the youngest captain of his local school's side at the age of sixteen years and three months.

A strapping two metres tall, with broad shoulders, he frightened the opposition with his run-up to the wicket and by the time the ball came out of his hand the batsman was already starting to think about taking evasive action.

His father had taught him the art of swing bowling and if the conditions were right, some of his deliveries were almost unplayable.

He regularly took five wickets in a match and boasted about bowling out all ten batsmen from the highly acclaimed local grammar school on one memorable balmy summer afternoon.

Academically he wasn't the brightest bulb in the room but with hard work and perseverance he managed to get the requisite "A" Level grades to get onto a graduate course with a top automotive company at their newly opened factory, just a fifteen-minute walk from his home.

Being a good-looking sportsman, having someone on his arm was not a problem but girls came and went as Jack was more of a "Man's Man", immature and far too young to think of settling down.

By the age of twenty-three Jack had his degree in engineering, was earning good money and it was time for him to leave home.

His father pulled a few strings at the local building society, helped out with the deposit and he was soon up and running on his own with a small, but new, semi-detached pad that he could call his own.

Quite when things started to go wrong it was difficult to pin down but being tall, well-built and possessing a fiery temper, was a potential recipe for disaster, particularly when combined with alcohol.

Jack couldn't hold his booze and his fists would start flying as soon as the alcohol level numbed his sense of reasoning. One night he went too far and ended up, as a guest, in the local police cells and was nearly charged with affray.

The following morning, he was cautioned by the magistrate and reminded that he could have ended up with a police record.

Nevertheless, with this slight blemish on his C.V., it wasn't the worst start for a twenty-three-year-old that hadn't been born with a silver spoon in his mouth.

He had a degree, a good solid job with huge promotion potential, a new house and above all a real passion for his beloved cricket.

Jack had followed in his father's footsteps and, after leaving school, joined the local cricket club that his father had captained for a number of years. The club known as Fieldhouses had been formed in 1928 and was on the outskirts of Wolverhampton in the West Midlands. It had been a member of the local league ever since its inception.

Having four divisions there had been regular promotion and relegation but the club had never quite managed a season in the Premier Division.

Apart from the regular weekend matches between Midland based clubs there was one special fixture that was everyone's favourite.

For many years there had been an annual match between Fieldhouses and a village side from Bundary on the outskirts of Bristol. The match was played on the Easter Bank Holiday Saturday with the teams taking it in turn to host the event.

Quite how the fixture had started in the first place was somewhat of a mystery but it had continued for at least twenty years and the matches were fiercely contested.

The players usually lodged with the opposing team members and over the years some had become quite friendly.

9

This particular year with Easter falling early, the match was to be played over the weekend of the 31st March/1st April.

It was Bundary's turn to host the match and Jack was looking forward to once again visiting his opposite number and opening bowler Danny Maguire.

Jack had met Danny two years before when he took over the captaincy for the first time. The real reason he was so excited, however, was that he had taken a real shine to Danny's wife Helen and following the weekend meeting, they had started a clandestine affair, which was starting to become quite serious.

He didn't feel too ashamed at coming onto a mate's wife, as Helen had made most of the running. But there was no denying the chemistry that existed between them.

As soon as they had clasped eyes on each other a basic instinct seemed to take over and whenever the opportunity presented itself, they couldn't keep their hands off each other.

They both knew that what they were doing was wrong but the basic animal attraction was too strong to resist. They had continued to keep in touch with each other by regular phone calls and text messages.

Danny sold industrial diamonds for a living and as his work took him all around the country, there were several opportunities for Jack and Helen to meet up.

This normally involved a lunch somewhere between Bristol and Wolverhampton but back in January they had managed to spend a night together at a romantic hotel in the Cotswold's and the bond between them had grown stronger.

The thought of seeing Helen once again caused butterflies to well up in his stomach as Jack drove to the cricket club for the first net practice of the year. His head was in a spin as he contemplated the visit to Bundary, which was now only a few weeks away.

Jack spotted his vice-captain Paul Ramsbottom across the car park and ambled over to meet him.

'All ready for the coming season, Rambo, I can't believe it has come round again so quickly.'

'Oh, hi, skip, just about got through winter without too many coughs and sneezes, but boy am I looking forward to playing some cricket, I must have put on at least half a stone.'

'Yep,' Jack replied. 'Do you realise its only four weeks until Easter and our match down at Bundary?'

Finally tugging his kitbag from the boot of the car Rambo caught up with Jack.

'Yes, I know,' said Rambo. 'We've got to get in some serious practice before the big match, we don't want to lose for a third time on the bounce.'

Jack examined the condition of the nets that had wintered quite well considering the amount of rain that had fallen, albeit the surface was covered in a thin film of mould which badly needing attention.

The bowling machine was wheeled out but the boys decided not to use it, as they desperately needed to get their bowling arms loose.

The rest of the team slowly arrived and with lots of "high fives" practice finally got under way.

Many people believed that cricket was much like baseball in that a ball was bowled as fast as possible at the batsman who then tried to smash it as hard as he possibly could.

Certainly, in recent years with the introduction of limited overs cricket, the game had changed and lost a lot of the intrigue that existed in a five day "test match".

There had always been rivalry between bowlers and batsmen, both claiming to be the most important part of the team.

For sure they required different skill sets with batsmen needing good eyesight, fast reactions and good hand and eye co-ordination.

Bowling, on the other hand, was somewhat more nuanced with fast bowlers learning the art of "swing" with subtle changes in the way the ball was held and the seam aligned at the point of delivery.

Spin bowling, however, was far more complicated with off-breaks, on-breaks, Googlies and the China-Man!

These were names that flummoxed anyone but the ardent cricket fan.

Jack's mother had watched cricket for thirty years but still did not claim to understand the rules. Why six balls in an over? And why was it called a maiden over when no runs were scored?

The fielding positions were even more bizarre with silly mid-on, silly mid-off, short fine leg and deep cover point!

It was not surprising that so many people did not understand the rules of cricket and the strange terminology that had evolved over the years since the game's invention.

Whilst Jack and Rambo were the opening bowlers, Mitch Johnson (Jonners) and Simon Wolf (Wolfie) were the opening batsmen. Both in their mid-twenties, they had played for Fieldhouses since leaving school and had slowly improved their batting averages with each passing season.

The wicket keeper "Mike the Cat Freeman" batted at number three and was the team chatterbox. From behind the stumps, apart from keeping wicket, his other role was to encourage the team and was consistently in trouble with the umpires for "sledging" the opposition.

Four further batsmen and two spin bowlers completed the side and for a small club with limited local talent they punched above their weight and fielded a half decent side. At the end of the two-hour training session Jack called the boys together.

'Right, guys, thanks for turning up tonight, it's great to see that everyone has survived our miserable winter – I don't need to tell you that our opening match against Bundary is less than four weeks away.

'I've been in touch with their match secretary who has given me the names on their team sheet and I have a list of their phone numbers and email addresses.

'Their team is the same as last year, as is ours, so you will be rooming with the same guys that you put up. I just hope that their pigsties are less smelly than yours!

'Can I ask you out of courtesy to make contact with your opposite numbers just to make sure we have ticked all the boxes? We are meeting in the local pub near Bundary called "The Wet Whistle" at 7.30 p.m. on Good Friday.

'We are taking four cars and we can get all the cricket gear and our own stuff in the back of Wolfie's SUV.

'OK, who's up for a curry at the Zanzibar?' Jack asked no one in particular.

The Zanzibar was the favourite curry house in town, although why an Indian restaurant was named after an African country left a question mark hanging in the air. Maybe the reason was that Zanzibar was famous for spices and the owner thought it had exotic connections. For sure Wolverhampton was blessed with an abundance of curry houses that had sprung up as the Indian community had grown substantially since the 1960s.

Jack's standard fare was a chicken tikka balti, madras hot, with boiled rice, three popadums and washed down with a couple of pints of lager.

As Jack set off for the curry house, he had a spring in his step; life was good at the moment and hopefully about to get better at the weekend when he would meet up again with Helen.

On the surface, Jack appeared to be the perfect son of much-loved parents, good looking and a good sportsman with a bright future ahead of him.

The picture, was not, however, as rosy as it seemed.

Unbeknown to his family and fellow teammates, there was a much darker side to Jack than anyone knew. When he was twenty-one years old, he had got involved with a crowd that was dabbling in recreational drugs. It had started with smoking "dope" but had quickly graduated onto taking cocaine and before long he was becoming hooked on the drug and needed a regular fix to keep him going.

He had met a friend, who knew a friend, who knew a friend who had supplied him with a quantity of cocaine that he had started using and found that if he cut it with baking soda, he could sell it to his mates and double his money.

The strength of the resulting mixture was obviously reduced but nevertheless still seemed to satisfy an ever-increasing demand for a weekend high.

He was very careful to make sure that he knew all his customers and could trust them with his shady little business on the side.

He knew it was illegal but *What the hell,* he thought, a little extra money really helped when you were a cash-strapped young man.

No one was going to be interested in a two-bit low-level guy who was dealing a bit of "Charlie" to help his mates out.

He justified it to himself by refusing to get involved in other drugs such as heroin or crystal meth on the basis that he was just selling party drugs that he thought should be on the N.H.S.

He knew that his parents would kill him if they were aware of what he was up to. He figured that he was just fulfilling a role, and if not, someone else would be doing it in his place. What he didn't realise was that very quickly he was becoming immersed in the murky world of drug dealing. The customer numbers started to increase as the word got round that Jack was the go-to man for the desired product.

Over the months as Jack's little business continued to grow, demand soon outstripped supply and he couldn't rely on a regular delivery from the dealer he used.

Out of the blue, the week before the cricket season was due to start, he received a telephone call from the main supplier who lived in the Birmingham area and asked if he would like to meet up to talk about improvement in distribution.

A meeting was arranged in The Swan pub car park near Edgbaston just outside of the city centre.

'I will be driving a black Porsche Panamera and I shall arrive at exactly 8.00 p.m. so do not be late,' were the only instructions Jack received.

Convinced that the man had an East European accent, Jack was intrigued to know what sort of background check had been done on himself before being allowed into a drug gang's inner circle.

He was aware that drug dealers were notoriously careful with whom they mixed and were constantly paranoid of being picked up by the police. He could only imagine that because he had been selling drugs for a couple of years without being caught, he was considered a fairly safe bet.

He arrived at the pub twenty minutes early and sure enough at exactly 8.00 p.m. the Porsche Panamera appeared out of the blue and pulled up at the far end of the car park.

The driver beckoned Jack to the passenger seat and somewhat nervously he got into the car.

Extending his hand Nikolay spoke first.

'Nikolay Agapov, and I am pleased to meet you, Jack Reed.'

His handshake was firm, yet not ridiculously vice like, the accent was most definitely East European and with a name like Nikolay Agapov almost certainly somewhere in The Balkans or maybe even Russia.

For the first few minutes they talked about their favourite cars and the relative differences between, Aston Martin, Mercedes and Porsche.

Having broken the ice Nikolay seemed keen to get down to business.

'Jack, I have noticed that your orders have increased significantly over the last few months and you have built up a very substantial network of users in the Wolverhampton area.

'Our business has also increased over the last year or so and we now supply drugs to the major cities of London, Birmingham, Manchester and Bristol through four main operatives.

'It is my job to ensure that those four operatives receive regular supplies and I in turn receive regular income. With each operative supplying about ten dealers, our network now employs some forty people.

'You, for example are one of twelve operatives here in the Midlands that are supplied by our Birmingham agent. For some time, we have been looking for someone that could run our U.K. operation and handle the collection and distribution of the drugs to our agents.'

He made the job specification sound like something that might appear in the Financial Times and appeared very blaze about the whole business.

The fact that he was talking about the sale and distribution of Class A drugs that could land them both in prison for many years didn't seem to bother him in the slightest.

Jack was intrigued.

'You mention handling your U.K. operation. Does that mean you have distribution elsewhere?'

Nikolay thought long and hard before replying but admitted that they had a drug distribution network that extended throughout most of Europe.

'Your job, Jack, would be very simple. You would fly half a dozen times a year to our base in The Balkans, deposit the money from our operatives, then return to Britain with four kilos of cocaine travelling by train through Europe. Travelling, as a back-packer on the train without a suitcase, would draw far less attention to you than if you risked going by plane. Getting through customs would be a lot easier. It is a wonderful scenic journey back to the U.K. that would take a couple of days.

'You would then deliver one kilo to each operative who would cut the pure cocaine with the same amount of baking powder or a similar additive, doubling what he started with. Today cocaine with strength of around fifty per cent fetches about fifty quid per gram on the street.

'Every journey means that both the operatives and us end up making a couple of hundred thousand quid each. What a fantastically fair business model.

'In total it would add up to over a million pounds worth of business a year.

'You know the crazy thing is, Jack, that laundering the cash is more difficult than obtaining the drugs.

'Fortunately, we have a stake in a local Balkan bank that can distribute all the money through a complicated exchange mechanism with other commercial banks and we now don't have a problem.

'Obviously, you would be taking risks every time you travelled but the train route from Belgrade to London is incredibly busy all year round with tourists from all over Europe.

'As I said, custom controls are far laxer on trains than at airports and we have had no problems over the last couple of years.

'The really good thing is that you can vary the route you take by either going via Budapest, Vienna, Cologne and Brussels or from Belgrade through Zagreb, Zurich and Paris.

'And if you really fancied a change, you could always take a ferry across to Bari then go by train up through Milan, Turin and Paris.

'The train journey takes a couple of days to get you back into London but the overnight sleeper accommodation is first class and the scenery is terrific.

'A journey like that is not exactly a hardship every other month.'

Jack realised that Nikolay had thought of everything but why would he trust someone like himself who he hardly knew?

'Why me, Nikolay? Why do you think you can trust me to do this job when you hardly know me?'

'We have done our research, Jack, we know everything about you. You do not have a police record; you have good standing in the local community and you are young and ambitious. You have managed to keep your little business secret from your friends and family, which is no mean achievement. I also understand that you have been put on for a short time at the automotive company, so no doubt you are finding your mortgage repayments difficult to meet.

'You have your own home in the West Midlands, which is a great central base from which to store and distribute the drugs.

'Living in the West Midlands puts you right at the heart of our operation. Being single also limits the amount of people passing through your home.

'You have been selling drugs for a couple of years now without being caught and as far as we know you are not on any police radar.

'You would have to make six trips every year and we will pay you twenty thousand pounds per trip, into an overseas bank account of your choice adding up to one hundred and twenty thousand pounds per year. We can also give you really good advice on which foreign bank to use without questions being asked about where the money originated.'

Jack couldn't really believe what he was hearing. Twenty minutes ago, he was hoping to meet someone who could guarantee him his regular supply of drugs and now he was being offered a job that could set him up for life.

The downside was, however, equally mind blowing. If he was caught shipping "Class A" drugs in quantity, he would be spending a lot of time in prison.

He had done his homework on the risks of peddling drugs such as cocaine and the average prison sentence for being caught with five kilos or less was just under eight years.

Five kilos was seen as an important threshold because convictions in cases of trafficking over five kilos carried a much greater average prison term of eleven years and six months.

Carrying four kilos in a backpack was the equivalent of carrying four bags of sugar, so it was doable without attracting too much attention.

The illegal drug industry throughout the world was massive and he remembered reading that fifty per cent of the prison population in Latin America was related to drug crime. The market was also growing rapidly with global annual production of cocaine estimated at over two thousand tonnes per year and although notoriously difficult to estimate, the worldwide cocaine market was thought to be worth about the same as heroin at one hundred billion dollars.

The total global market for all illegal drugs was now estimated to be in excess of five hundred billion dollars.

Jack was old enough and wise enough to understand the seriousness of the industry that he was involved in. The problem was that like most dealers he never thought that he would get caught.

All sorts of thoughts were flying around in his head when Nikolay made a suggestion.

'Look, Jack, you do not have to make a decision today. Why don't you give it some thought and if you think it is something you are up for, we could fly out to the Balkans and you can meet the rest of the team.

'Obviously until you decide what you want to do, I cannot give you too much information on our network. But I can assure you that we are extremely professional and you will be mightily impressed with our people and the security of our operation.

'We are a very tight knit family and we run a very small operation in comparison to some of the Balkan gangs. Our future depends very much on secrecy and trust and if you become part of the family, we would expect total and absolute loyalty.

'A Serbian family of two brothers own the business and in addition to them there is a distribution director, a finance director and a procurement director.'

Jack thought that the board of directors sounded more like a public company than a drug operation based in the Balkans!

Nikolay continued.

'There are only a couple of dozen people who work exclusively within the network and that allows us close supervision and control of the whole operation.

'If the authorities caught you with drugs, there would be no support from us and we would deny any knowledge of involvement with you. For obvious reasons all our people must have a clean police record.

'To earn the sort of money you are looking at does not come without risks and you have to weigh up whether you are prepared for that sort of life or not.'

Jack punched Nikolai's contact number into his phone and sensed that the meeting was now at an end.

He suggested that with Easter being just a couple of weeks away he would like to use that time to think over things and would get back to Nikolay one way or another.

They shook hands and within seconds the Porsche Panamera was racing off into busy streets of downtown Birmingham.

As Jack got back into his car, his head was spinning with all sorts of thoughts but in spite of all the attractions the job had to offer, he knew that in reality the risks were too great. There was a world of difference between earning a little extra money on the side, and risking maybe a couple of years inside, compared to getting caught up in an international drug smuggling operation that may land him a prison sentence in excess of ten years.

As he turned left out of the car park, his mind was pretty much made up that it was probably time to get back to living in the real world and concentrate on earning an honest living.

He was far too preoccupied to spot the grey Volvo Estate parked in the small cul de sac opposite.

Jack may have thought that his little business would fly under the radar of any drug enforcement operation but he was completely wrong.

He had been under surveillance by the drug squad division of the West Midlands Police for a number of months and it was one of their officers who had been taking photographs of the meeting held between Jack and the mysterious man in the Porsche Panamera.

It only took a phone call to the head office to reveal that the number plate of the Porsche was registered to a Nikolay Agapov. The name had a red flag alongside it that indicated he was a person of extreme interest to the West Midland drug law enforcement department.

As his thoughts turned to Helen and the impending Easter cricket match at Bundary on the outskirts of Bristol, he was blissfully unaware that he was getting deeper and deeper into a potentially far more dangerous ball game than cricket.

Chapter Two

After two more cricket-training sessions, the boys felt that most of the rust accumulated over the cold winter months had all but disappeared.

As the weather started to improve and with Easter just round the corner, there was growing confidence in the team that this could be their year to shine.

Good Friday finally arrived and everyone was excited at the prospect of the opening match of the season.

They set off for Bundary in glorious sunshine and rather than try to drive in convoy they agreed to meet up at the "Wet Whistle" no later than 7.00 p.m.

Needless to say, the journey down the M5 motorway was exactly as expected, a complete nightmare.

It was as if road works were actually installed to frustrate holidaymakers rather than to help them.

A five-mile tailback had started just south of Bromsgrove only to be followed by an accident near Cheltenham that resulted in two lanes being completely closed and all the holiday traffic being funnelled into one horrendously long queue.

Eventually the logjam dispersed and everyone arrived in good time to meet up with the Bundary players.

There were lots of man hugs and backslapping as the players mingled with each other and began to discuss their respective chances of winning the forthcoming match.

Jack spotted his opposite number Danny at the bar and made a beeline for him.

'Danny, how the devil are you?'

'I can see that your looks haven't improved over this last twelve months. No doubt your bowling hasn't either.'

'Now don't you start winding me up before the weekend has even started, Jack, you may find you haven't got a bed to sleep in unless you are nice to me.'

The mention of bed immediately set Jack off in another direction.

'Is Helen still making an honest man out of you, Danny, or has she moved onto greener pastures?'

'No, we are still together but God knows why as we seem to spend most of our time arguing rather than having a good time.'

'I'm sorry to hear that, Danny, life is too short for all that sort of nonsense.'

Secretly, of course, Jack was delighted that not everything in the garden was rosy. He had plans to make Helen happier than she had ever imagined.

'So, listen up, boys!' Danny shouted across the bar.

'The plan tonight is for you all to drop your kit off at your respective places, have a quick freshen-up and then it's over to my place for a barbecue. It looks as though the weather is going to hold so hopefully, we shall have a great evening.'

Wolfie couldn't help butting in.

'I have nightmares if I sleep on my own, is there any chance Simon will let me sleep with his wife?'

Quick as a flash Simon replied.

'I'd let you sleep in the kitchen with our bulldog but he's a bit choosy these days and isn't too keen on smelly "Black Country Boys" from the West Midlands.'

The banter continued until Danny suggested it was time to make a move before everyone forgot what was next on the agenda.

'We can pick up some drinks at the garage on the way to my place, so if you want to follow me, I suggest some of our lads come with you and vice versa so that nobody gets lost on the way back.'

Having thrown his kit into the boot, Jack jumped into the car alongside Danny and they set off for the garage.

'Anything in particular, Danny?' Jack enquired.

'No, just a dozen or so tinnies from the fridge should do you and me. The others can get what they like.'

Danny's house came into view and was literally a stone's throw away from the Bundary cricket ground.

Jack asked whether Danny had planned to buy somewhere so close to the cricket ground for convenience or was it just how things had turned out.

'Oh no,' Danny replied. 'It just happened to be on the market when Helen and I were looking for somewhere. It ticked all the boxes and seemed to make a lot of sense when our lives were going to be involved with the club for the foreseeable future.'

As the car pulled onto the drive, Jack's heart started to pound in anticipation of seeing Helen once again.

The light came on in the hall and as she opened the door Jack was taken aback by what he saw. She looked truly stunning with her hair that was swept back in a ponytail that seemed to exaggerate the simplicity of her stunning looks.

'I said, do you want to bring your kitbag in now or later?' Danny asked.

Jack realised that he had been staring at Helen and had not heard a word that Danny had said.

'No, I'll bring in it now if that's OK.'

As Helen moved towards him, Jack looked into her deep blue eyes and realised in that very moment that he was actually in love with her.

She leant forward to kiss him on the cheek but the kiss fell onto his lips as if guided by something beyond their control. As he held her head, her beautiful long blond hair felt incredibly soft between his hands. Holding each other's gaze for a few seconds, Jack felt a knot tighten in his stomach and he realised that this was something special.

Helen showed Jack to his room and with Danny ferrying in food from the car she had another opportunity to be alone with him.

She threw her arms around his neck and pulled him close to her.

'I can't tell you how much I have looked forward to seeing you again,' she whispered as he kissed her gently on the back of her neck.

'We have to be careful,' Jack said. 'But I have a plan which will allow me to see you tomorrow for an hour or so. We can discuss it later at the barbecue. For the meantime you had better get going downstairs before Danny begins to smell a rat.

'I am going to have a quick shower and change of clothes but give me twenty minutes and I shall be straight down.'

The rest of the boys slowly arrived and by 8.30 p.m. the party was in full swing. A few of the Bundary players had brought their wives/girlfriends along to help with the food but with twenty-two hungry men to feed it was difficult to keep the burgers and sausages on the barbecue long enough to be cooked.

Everyone seemed to be getting along and as the booze continued to flow the level of conversation seemed to increase.

There were another couple of trips to the garage to top up on supplies but as the evening wore on, the level of consumption finally slowed down.

Trying not to appear too obvious, Helen inched towards Jack and finally got his attention.

'So, what's this plan you have in mind for us to meet up tomorrow then?' she whispered.

'Well, if for example Bundary bat first, I will obviously not be able to escape because I shall be out on the field of play for the whole innings. But when it is our turn to bat I shall have at least a couple of hours in which I can disappear because I am the last man to go into bat for our team.

'I can go for a walk around the boundary and then disappear out of the car park before crossing the field to your place, which should take exactly five minutes. I will send you a text as soon as I know what time I can make it.'

Helen made the point that she could make any time after about 2.30 p.m. and disappeared into the kitchen just as Wolfie came over with half a barbecued sausage in his one hand and a can of lager in the other.

'Hi, skip, have we been lucky with the weather or have we been lucky with weather! There is no rain forecast for the whole weekend which is lucky because I've known it to snow when Easter has been this early in the year.'

'Too right, Wolfie, cricket is one of those games that is fantastic when the weather is good and bloody awful when it is raining and cold. I've spent too many hours in my life staring out at rainclouds and wondering when they will disappear.'

As time wore on and with the temperature dropping, people began moving into the kitchen to avoid the chill evening breeze that was starting to spring up in the garden.

Danny, who had been working the barbecue, was glad to escape the heat and ambled over to Jack and Wolfie.

'Well, that's all the food gone. Four dozen sausages, two dozen chicken breasts and the same number of burgers. Doesn't anyone ever get fed in your neck of the woods?'

'Well, I think it's the smell of the barbecue and eating outside that makes it special.' Wolfie chipped in.

Someone turned on the music system in the lounge and before long the dancing had started albeit with a shortage of any sort of skill or rhythm.

In addition to the eleven cricketers, Fieldhouses had brought along their own scorer Alison Bunfield (known to the players as Bunny).

Scoring was an incredibly important part of a cricket match and Bunny was the best in the business. She had become interested in scoring whilst watching her brother play for the Fieldhouses youth side. By the age of ten she understood how to enter all the different hand signals from the umpires, this included; byes, leg byes, wides, no-balls, runs scored and all manner of other weird signals that had evolved over 100 years or more and were specific to the game of cricket.

The two on-field umpires would signal from the field of play to the scorers in the scorebox and every detail of the match would be entered into a pre-printed scorebook.

This was so complicated that it looked more like a manual for a space flight rather than something devised to record the events of a cricket match.

Bunny, who was in her mid-twenties, was staying with the Bundary scorer Sarah Miles at her flat just outside the village.

Sarah who was in her early thirties, had just gone through a messy divorce and had taken up scoring for the club as a sort of hobby that got her out of the flat and gave her the opportunity of meeting some eligible bachelors.

'Well, that was the idea,' she said to Bunny. 'But have you seen this load of tosspots? There isn't one bloke I would dream of hooking up with.

'I haven't been scoring long, Bunny, so I am hoping that you can help me with all the finer points. It really is the most complicated game in the world to understand.'

'Like all things in life, simple when you know how,' Bunny replied.

As the Bose speakers continued to thump out the music Bunny and Sarah decided to make a move and head for the sack.

It was after midnight and getting to the point where most men turned into boys and started the silly drinking games.

Wolfie and Jonners had got into a debate with two of the Bundary boys about how many village cricket sides were folding.

'The problem is one of time,' Wolfie suggested. 'It used to be a wonderful family occasion when the ladies would make the teas, the kids would play each other and everyone would get together after the match for a drink or two.'

'The Drink Driving law ruined all that,' Jonners added.

'Nowadays people take the game far too seriously and it has become mega competitive. I am sure the players do not get the enjoyment out of it they used to.'

Slowly and surely the party thinned out and at midnight Danny announced that it was time to call it a day.

'Come on, you lot, it's time to head for home. Unless you had forgotten, we have an important cricket match tomorrow and I don't want you nursing hangovers all day long.'

Animated discussions were still raging about all manner of things and like most opinions, when drink was involved, feelings were running high.

Wolfie and Jonners were having an argument about the local golf club they had recently joined. Jonners felt that golf was still the province of the select few and couldn't understand why he had to go through an interview for selection.

'I didn't have to go through a bloody interview when I joined Fieldhouses so what's so special about membership to a golf club,' he contested.

'Well, what's wrong with having a look at you to make sure that you fit in with the rest of the members?' Wolfie replied.

Jack took the opportunity to usher the pair out the door.

'You pair can finish this argument in the car. It's a miracle the golf club accepted you both in the first place. They must be getting desperate for members if you two got in without too much trouble.'

Eventually the stragglers were rounded up and sent packing leaving just Helen, Danny and Jack to tidy up and collect all the rubbish.

'Helen, why don't you leave all this until tomorrow, I'm absolutely bushwhacked and need to get to bed,' Danny suggested.

'You know that I hate leaving mess until the following morning. You get to bed; I'm sure Jack will collect all the empty cans and bottles for me.'

'Jack's our guest for the weekend, Helen, you can't expect him to help with the clearing up.'

'Danny, it is absolutely no problem at all to me,' Jack insisted.

'I've always been a night owl, so it will suit me to chill out and help Helen get the house back in some sort of order.'

The reality, of course, was completely different as Jack was just desperate to be alone with Helen so that they could spend some more time together.

'OK, have it your way, Jack,' Danny said with a somewhat tired and resigned look on his face and with that he disappeared up the stairs.

Jack opened up a black bin liner bag and started filling it with all the empties. He couldn't believe how many cans had been consumed and what a mess a couple of dozen people could make in just a few hours.

Eventually with glasses in the dishwasher, the rubbish put outside and the music turned down, the job of tidying up was all but done.

Listening for any movement in the upstairs bedroom, Jack pulled Helen towards him. He was filled with an excitement that he had never experienced before and he felt lost in a world of lust and anticipation.

His hands were all over her and he could feel her tight buttocks through the flimsy summer dress that she was wearing.

His right hand instinctively moved to the inside of her thigh and she started moaning as he moved further up her legs.

Any minute she is going to stop me, Jack thought.

But she didn't stop him; as he reached the top of her legs, he could feel that her small cotton pants were wringing wet with desire.

He slid his fingers inside her and she groaned with an intensity that only happens when passions reach such a height.

His erection wanted to burst out of his trousers as she started to tug at the buckle on his belt.

At the last minute he grabbed her arms.

'Helen, Helen, stop, please stop, we can't do this, not here anyway, not tonight. What happens if Danny hears us and comes downstairs?'

'I don't care if he comes downstairs, I have got to have your body, I have got to have you inside me. I have never felt like this in my life and I am going to trust my feelings rather than regret missing something I know is so right.'

She started crying, but she insisted that they were tears of joy not sadness and as she began to calm down, she turned to Jack and with mascara running down her cheeks she continued.

'Jack, you have no idea how unhappy I am, there is nothing left between Danny and myself, we have had issues which I don't want to go into now but it has left us in a loveless marriage. There is nothing wrong with him as a person, he looks after me, is kind to me but the spark that was once there has gone. Everything has become a chore rather than a pleasure and when he comes home at night, we struggle to find anything to talk about.

'Quite frankly I have just become bored, and maybe Danny has too. This last year has been the worst year of my life.

'I cannot stop thinking about our night in the Cotswold's in January and how close we were. That is how people of our age should feel, Jack, excited, sexual and wanting to be together. Life passes by so quickly that I don't want to miss any opportunity to be happy.

'I have to tell you that I have been having an affair with someone else since we first met but that has all gone horribly wrong as well.

'Please, Jack, please understand that I cannot go on like this and I need to get away. I will come and live with you in the West Midlands and we can start a new life together.'

Jack suddenly started to sober up.

He realised that he was in a lot deeper than he had thought. He had no idea that Helen was so desperately sad and looking for a way out of her predicament.

He had to think all this through, after all they hadn't exactly spent a lot of time together and there was absolutely no certainty that they would make a go of it. He also knew that at the age of twenty-three he was probably too young to settle down.

Having said that he also knew that he was incredibly attracted to her and there was certainly a strong chemistry between them.

'There's something else, Jack, that you need to know, something that could get me into big trouble with the police. As you know I work part-time in the "Wet Whistle", the pub you all met in earlier on. Well, a lot of those regulars that you saw tonight are customers of mine for cocaine and other recreational drugs.

'What started as a bit of fun and an easy way to make some extra money on the side, has turned into somewhat of a fully blown business.

'Worst still I am now mixing with some really shady characters. These are thoroughly nasty people who are only interested in money and would stop at nothing in the pursuit of it.

'The guy that I have been having an affair with is the drug dealer that I have been getting the goods from and we were planning to run away together.

'But just recently I started to get cold feet and realised that I wasn't in love with him at all and then.'

Helen's voice tailed off as she started to sob uncontrollably.

'Jack, I have to tell you that I am eight weeks pregnant and the dates just happen to coincide with when we met up in January.

'He knows that I am pregnant and I haven't the heart to tell him that the baby may not be his. He knows nothing about our affair and would kill me if he thought I had been to bed with someone else.

'He is incredibly jealous and now that I am pregnant, he is even more determined than ever for us to run away together and is equally determined that I should keep the baby.

'He has become aggressive and when I suggested that maybe I should get rid of the baby, he went berserk and reminded me that it was his baby as well as mine and that I can't just choose to get rid of it without his consent.

'We were planning to leave just after Easter but I don't want to run away with him and have this child not knowing whether it is his or yours, it just isn't right.

'Jack, please take me back to Wolverhampton with you. I will do whatever you want me to do. You could have a paternity test and if the baby is yours, we can start a family together away from all this madness. If the baby is not yours, I promise you that I will have an abortion.'

Jack didn't feel it was the right time to admit that he had a similar drug scam running in his hometown and had just received a job offer that would make any commitment extremely difficult.

He was also not convinced that he wanted to take on the responsibility of a baby at the age of twenty-three.

It was after 1.00 a.m. when Jack finally convinced Helen that it was time to call it a day.

'We can discuss what we should do when I come round tomorrow during the cricket match. I think its best we sleep on it for the time being and then take it from there.'

Helen starting crying again but just as she was about to speak Jack thought he heard a noise from upstairs.

There was one last embrace in the kitchen before they kissed each other good night and with that Jack wearily found the way to his bedroom.

By the time he collapsed on the bed, he had well and truly sobered up and couldn't believe what a day it had been. It had all started with the simple pleasure of looking forward to a cricket match over a Bank Holiday weekend and had finished with the possibility of running off with the opposing captain's wife who could well be pregnant with his child.

That would not go well with his teammates, his parents or anyone else for that matter.

Was Helen a crazy mixed-up kid who had married too young and would now go from one disaster to another or could she be the partner he had always dreamed of meeting?

As he drifted off to sleep, he kept thinking about how excited he had been about seeing Helen again and what incredible chemistry existed between them.

It really had been one of the best days of his life.

What Jack did not realise was that tomorrow would be one of the worst days of his life.

Chapter Three

Jack blinked as the rays of a beautiful spring morning pierced the darkness of his bedroom. For a few seconds, he had no idea where he was, but as he slowly came round, the full reality of what had happened the night before began to dawn on him.

He couldn't believe that in just twenty-four hours his world had been turned upside down and he was now facing decisions that would affect the rest of his life.

How could he possibly know whether things would work out with Helen, did he want to settle down at this stage of his life with someone? What would his parents think? Could he cope with the fact that she was pregnant with a child that may or may not be his?

All these questions were running round his head as he tried to get some sort of perspective into the situation. At twenty-three years old Helen was the same age as Jack and as far as he knew she had been married for three years. He figured it was long enough for her to know whether the marriage was working but by the same token not long enough to call it a day without trying a little longer.

He had always believed that a man shouldn't settle down before he was thirty but here he was falling for someone who in all likelihood would be a divorcee by the tender age of twenty-three.

He wasn't sure whether he was ready to take on the responsibility of raising a family and all the commitment that went with it.

But he did know she was the first woman he had met that he had truly fallen for.

As he lay on the bed pondering all the pros and cons a wonderful smell of cooked bacon floated up the stairs.

He realised that he was extremely hungry.

Danny seemed to be in charge of cooking and the sight of sausages, bacon, mushrooms and tomato helped to lift his spirits as he settled down for a full English breakfast.

'Morning, Jack, I hope you slept well and many thanks for helping Helen out with all the tidying up. It looks as though we have dropped lucky with the weather and it's going to be a great day for our cricket match.'

Feeling incredibly guilty at what had happened the night before, Jack attempted to make as much small talk as he could.

'Do you know Helen and I cleared away over sixty empty cans and a dozen bottles of wine from last night? I can't believe how much people can drink. Let's hope it doesn't affect their performance on the field today.'

Helen appeared from nowhere and without making eye contact with Jack she started to lay the table for breakfast. There was an awkward silence that was eventually broken by Danny talking about the forthcoming match.

'So, we are having a fifty overs per side match starting at 1.00 p.m. with a break for tea at 4.00 p.m. Is that your understanding as well, Jack?'

'That's absolutely fine,' Jack replied as he tucked into his breakfast without any further delay.

Jack asked Danny how long Bundary cricket club had been in existence.

'Oh, Bundary was one of the founder members of the eighty-nine clubs that make up the Bristol & District Cricket League. The club was established in nineteen twenty-eight and has fielded at least two senior teams ever since. We also have an extremely active youth section, which is run by the director of cricket. He is the only paid member of the club, as everyone else is voluntary.

'Like most amateur teams the committee consists of about a dozen people who meet every month to discuss the main issues. The teams are predominately comprised of people living in the village but its catchment area does extend further afield nowadays.

'Helen, I bet you didn't know that the game of cricket started in Britain back in the sixteenth century and that most villages throughout the country can boast a ground that is the focal point of the local community during the spring and summer months. I also bet you didn't know that there are over six thousand amateur cricket teams that play cricket every year here in the UK.'

Helen really didn't care how many amateur cricket teams there were in England and proceeded to make some more toast.

After breakfast Danny disappeared to the local shop to pick up a weekend newspaper and it gave Jack the chance to talk to Helen about the plans for later.

'So, I'll text you with the time to expect me depending on whether I can get away. It will probably be sometime after 4.00 p.m. Are you happy with that?'

'Jack, I've got goosebumps just thinking about it, the sooner you can get here the better. Are you absolutely sure you want this? I don't want to be just another number on your list of conquests.'

'Helen, I keep telling you that I have never felt like this with any other woman in my life. I feel terrible that I am doing all this behind Danny's back but I promise that I won't let you down. We can talk later about where we go from here.'

Danny arrived back with the papers and the boys settled down to read whatever rubbish was hitting the headlines whilst Helen cleared away the remnants of breakfast.

The news was not really worth reading and Jack found it difficult to concentrate given that he was far more interested in what was going to happen later.

The clock moved on and it was soon time to gather up all the cricket clobber and drive the two-minute journey to the ground.

Helen had managed to get out of helping with the afternoon tea on the basis of her hosting the barbecue the night before.

'I shall chill out here all afternoon while you boys play bat and ball,' she said with somewhat of a sarcastic tone.

In reality, of course, she would be counting down the minutes until Jack arrived and then the fun would really begin.

Bundary cricket ground was in a stunning location comprising eight acres of lush green outfield with a central wicket that looked like a well-mown carpet. The wooden pavilion and scorebox was as traditional as it gets for village cricket and the mature oak trees surrounding the playing area completed the most picturesque setting anyone could have imagined.

Many village cricket grounds around Britain were over a hundred years old and therefore remained unspoilt and not subject to urban sprawl. Over the years birds would come back to the same nesting site and Bundary was famous for having a returning cuckoo.

For years, from April onwards, the sound of the cuckoo echoed around the ground and gave a wonderful backdrop to the beautiful setting of a village idyll.

It was really quite sad that having travelled from the forests of Africa all the way to England, the cuckoo never seemed to find a mate and in late June he returned home.

The rooms in the pavilion were fairly basic but functional and the lounge sported a long bar, which seemed to sell every imaginable brand of beer as well as some local "Real Ales".

A reasonable sized kitchen, a small committee room, home and away changing rooms and ladies and gents toilets completed the interior of the somewhat traditional cricket pavilion.

There were pictures of teams hanging on the walls that dated back throughout the history of the club and honorary boards that showed the names of the captains from the very first year the club was formed back in nineteen twenty-eight.

The players started to arrive in dribs and drabs and in fairness did not look to be suffering any ill effects from the night before.

With everyone changed into their "whites", Jack and Danny ventured onto the square for the traditional toss of a coin to decide who would have the choice of batting or bowling first.

The photographer from the local gazette followed them onto the pitch as the annual match always attracted a lot of interest within the local community.

It was the tradition for the visiting captain to make the call and having lost the toss, Danny decided that Bundary would bat first which meant that Jack would be out in the field until teatime and would be able to see Helen as planned.

Jack texted Helen to say that if all went well, he would be with her at about 4.30 p.m.

The ground was beginning to fill up as more and more people arrived. With it being Easter Saturday the Bundary/Fieldhouse's fixture was one of the village highlights of the year.

It was always a close match and families would turn up with their picnic baskets, deckchairs and children in tow in order to make a day of it.

The kids would set up their own game in the corner of the ground and take it in turns to bat and bowl.

Mothers with young children in prams and pushchairs would walk around the ground and the occasional passer-by would pass comment on how quickly the youngsters grew up from one year to the next.

This year a pig roast had been organised for the first time but the "Bouncy Castle" had been cancelled due to health and safety issues.

The ice cream van and raffle stall completed the attractions and with the weather looking settled for the day everyone looked forward to what they hoped would be a wonderful day.

As Jack marked out his run up to bowl the first over the sun finally broke through and they really couldn't have wished for a better Easter Saturday anywhere in the country.

The two umpires took up their positions on the field of play and when the two scorers Bunny and Sarah signalled that they were ready, play finally got under way just after 1.00 p.m.

Jack set a traditional field for an opening bowler with all the fielders in positions that sounded completely ridiculous except wicket keeper. Why deep square leg? Why gully? And why third man? Nobody really knew how the names of the positions on a cricket field had evolved throughout the years but they had remained the same for well over a century.

The first few overs passed without incident and after a dropped catch in the "slips", Bundary moved onto the respectable score of 40 without the loss of a single wicket.

"Mike The Cat" was getting frustrated behind the stumps as the batsmen seemed to be well settled.

'Anytime now, lads!' he shouted with encouragement and sure enough the very next ball Rambo bowled an absolute peach of a ball that took the middle stump right out the ground.

With two more wickets falling quickly, Bundary were suddenly 48 for the loss of three wickets and Fieldhouses were very much in the driving seat.

Batting became easier as the new ball lost its sheen and didn't move around so much in the air, as it had in the first half an hour of play.

Bundary reached 120 runs for the loss of one more wicket and at this stage the game was evenly poised.

Bundary's best batsman Bob Short had scored a half-century and looked in no trouble at all when a bizarre incident suddenly turned the game Fieldhouse's way.

As he leaned forward to play a shot he hit the back of his leading knee with the bat, promptly lost his balance and fell onto the pitch outside the batting crease.

Quick as a flash "Mike the Cat" whipped off the bails and now Bundary were 120 for the loss of five wickets but had lost their best batsmen and were in danger of being bowled out for a low score.

It was very rare for someone to be stumped by the wicket keeper and Mike was extremely pleased with the speed that he had executed the manoeuvre.

There was a mini revival before the next wicket fell and Bundary eventually limped to 180 for nine wickets when captain Danny came in to bat as the last man. He took a wild swing that sent the ball out of the ground and into the next field. With a big flourish the umpire signalled "six" to the scorers.

Unfortunately, he tried to execute exactly the same shot with the next ball, missed and his middle stump went flying out of the ground.

Bundary were finally all out just before 4.00 p.m. with a total on the scoreboard of 186 runs, which was considered to be slightly under par but nevertheless reasonably competitive.

It meant that tea could be taken a little early and Jack texted Helen again to say that he would be there by 4.15 p.m. and to leave the back door open for him.

Fieldhouses would start their innings at about 4.30 p.m. and unless they suffered a massive batting collapse Jack knew that he had at least a couple of hours to be with Helen and still get back in time to bat if needed. Hopefully Fieldhouses would knock off the runs without him needing to go out to bat at all.

It had always been the tradition of the club that the chairman's wife organised the teas for the special day and with a few of her friends from the local choir, they had put on a banquet that was fit for a king.

Afternoon tea at the Ritz in London may have taken some beating but afternoon tea at Bundary cricket ground on Easter Saturday certainly gave it a run for its money.

There were finger sandwiches with a choice of six different fillings, including the compulsory cucumber variety. There were homemade scones with clotted cream and strawberry or raspberry jam.

Then as if that wasn't enough the five ladies from the choir had all excelled by baking a range of cakes that were mouth-dribblingly irresistible and included Black Forest Gateau, Mango Meringue, Banana Cake with Cream Cheese frosting, Victoria Sponge and Lemon Drizzle.

Jack was far too excited to really appreciate the wonderful spread that was on offer and having downed a few sandwiches and a scone, he decided to make a move before the players returned to the pitch. He was far less likely to be missed if he left now rather than when the match started again.

He casually wandered to the back of the car park and making sure there was nobody watched he jumped over the fence and into the adjacent field. Helen's house was literally a five-minute walk across two fields. There was a small gate from the field into the back garden of the house, which the farmer had agreed to so that Danny could walk to the cricket club rather than drive.

46

With his heart pounding like a drum, he opened the back door of the house and expected Helen to come running towards him. Passing through the utility room he entered the kitchen calling her name but there was complete silence and as moved to the other side of the island kitchen unit he suddenly noticed her.

She was lying on the floor, slumped in a heap, with a large kitchen knife protruding from her abdomen and surrounded by a sea of blood.

His immediate reaction was to take the knife out of her stomach and throw it in the sink in some vain stupid hope that she would recover.

He stopped in his tracks for a few seconds realising that the knife would carry the fingerprints of the murderer but overcome by emotion and shock he could not stop himself from slowly removing the knife from her body.

Her arms and legs were pale and with her eyes wide open, she appeared to have a look of disbelief etched on her face. She would have realised very quickly that her lifeblood was literally draining away.

He suddenly felt sick and started retching uncontrollably over the sink as the enormity of the situation began to dawn on him.

Glancing around the kitchen he noticed that the place had been ransacked. Not a drawer had been left unopened and it appeared that whoever had perpetrated the crime had been looking for something.

As the retching subsided, Jack was hit by a tsunami of emotion and tears started to pour down his face. Her motionless body was everything that she was not. She had shone with vivacity and passion but now it was as though someone had pulled the plug on an electrifying life.

Jack started to shake as his brain slowly processed the shock of what he had witnessed. He couldn't think straight but he knew that he had to do something otherwise he was going to be the prime suspect.

His initial reaction was to get back to the cricket ground as quickly as possible and hope that it was all just a bad dream. He didn't want to believe what he had seen and suddenly he was in complete denial. This sort of thing only happened in films, not in real life.

He sat down on a chair and stared into space; he couldn't bring himself to look at her. All the hopes and dreams of a future life together had disappeared into a dark pool of blood that seemed to be covering most of the kitchen floor.

And the baby, oh my God, the baby has died with her. How could anybody have done this?

Another wave of emotion flowed over his body and he suddenly felt very cold as if his own blood was draining away as well.

Then he realised that his DNA would be all over the murder scene, her blood was on his shoes.

But he had done nothing wrong.

As he came to his senses, he realised that there was no option but to phone the police. The sooner they could get to the murder scene, the sooner they could start looking for the evil culprit.

He took a deep breath and dialled 999.

Once put through to the police with tears rolling down his face, he uttered the words he would never forget.

'I need to report the murder of a beautiful young woman.

'She has been stabbed to death at her home here at No 23 Winslow Gardens, Bundary. Please get someone here as soon as possible.'

Chapter Four

Although it seemed an eternity, it was probably only a few minutes before Jack could hear a police siren getting ever closer. He stared at Helen's lifeless body and although he knew the human body only held eight pints of blood, he couldn't believe how much of it seemed to have spread so far.

The normal bright red colour was slowly congealing into a sticky crimson mess and there was a sort of acrid smell hanging in the air.

The police hammered on the front door and in an act of futile respect Jack asked the two officers to come in through the back door, as he didn't want to traipse through the hall with his blood-stained cricket boots.

'So, what's going on here young man and why are you dressed in cricket whites?' said the officer who seemed even younger than Jack.

'I would prefer to tell you the whole story down at the station, I think the main priority is to show some dignity to Helen and get the pathologist here as quickly as possible.' Jack replied.

'So, you know this woman then?' the second officer quizzically asked.

'Yes, yes of course I know her, I was staying here last night as a guest of Bundary's cricket captain Danny Maguire and I had arranged to meet her this afternoon.'

Jack's explanation tailed off as he realised the explanation was not going to make any sense to the two men. The senior officer was working his radio and asking for backup as well as asking the station to arrange for the pathologist to be contacted.

'I think the sooner we can secure this place as a crime scene the sooner we can get the body moved to the mortuary,' he suggested with some authority.

It was obvious that both officers were shocked by the sight of Helen lying in a pool of blood and weren't sure of what to do next. There had probably never been a murder in the village and certainly they had never come across such a gruesome scene.

Jack was led away and put in the police car just as the crime investigation force arrived en masse.

There was some discussion as to whether he should be handcuffed but after a brief discussion with headquarters he was spared the indignity, at least for the time being. The cul de sac came to life as every man and his dog seemed to appear out of thin air wondering what on earth had happened.

The entire house was sealed off with the normal yellow tape used in crime scenes and a police officer was stationed at the front door ensuring that only suitably dressed officers in their standard white outfits could enter.

The forensic team duly arrived in full force and the photographer started taking pictures of the crime scene as the fingerprint experts got to work with their normal efficiency.

Tongues really started wagging when a non-descript burgundy van arrived and the body of Helen Maguire was eventually brought out for transportation to the morgue for further forensic investigation.

Staring out of the police car window, Jack was suddenly shocked back into reality when his phone started ringing.

'Jack, this is Rambo, where on earth are you? We have been looking all around the ground for you. Wickets are tumbling and you are the next man in to bat.'

Jack suddenly went cold as he realised that no one at the ground had a clue about what had happened.

'Rambo, there is no easy way of telling you this but Danny's wife has been stabbed and murdered and I'm currently in a police car on the way to Bristol's main police station. The poor girl was lying in a pool of blood with a huge kitchen knife stuck in her abdomen.'

His voice tailed off as the emotion started to get to him.

'You are going to have to call off the match as the police are on the way to the cricket ground to inform Danny.'

'Jack, if this is some sort of sick joke, I am not in the slightest bit amused,' growled Rambo.

Through a flood of tears Jack assured Rambo that it was certainly not a joke but at that point his mobile phone was taken off him.

Rambo was about to approach the umpires on the field of play to abandon the match just as the police car arrived at the ground. He approached the two officers and explained that he was the vice-captain of the team and he had just taken a call from Jack informing him of the situation.

Rambo was visibly shaken as the officers filled him in with what sketchy information they had.

It was obvious that Jack was involved in some way as he had discovered the body but what was he doing at the house in the middle of a cricket match?

There were so many unanswered questions that had Rambo completely baffled.

'I'm afraid, sir, we are going to have to stop the match because we need to speak to the murdered girl's husband as soon as possible,' the police officer said in an officious tone.

'Yes, yes, I completely understand,' replied Rambo and as the over being bowled had just been completed, all three men walked swiftly onto the field of play and approached the somewhat bemused umpires.

One of the police officers explained to the umpires why the match had to be stopped and asked if everyone could leave the field of play. The Bundary players were devastated as they only needed to take another two wickets and they would have won the match.

There was total confusion, as the spectators couldn't understand what could possibly have happened to warrant a police presence and an abandonment of the match.

The officers then approached Danny and ushered him to one side to create a degree of privacy.

'I'm afraid we have some extremely bad news. Mr Maguire, it appears that earlier this afternoon someone broke into your house and following a possible struggle, your wife was fatally murdered.

'The body was discovered by Jack Reed and he is currently helping us with our enquiries.'

'What on earth was Jack doing at my house in the middle of the cricket match?' Danny understandably asked.

But before the officer could say a word, the penny began to drop and Danny was the first to answer his own question.

'There's only one possible reason why he would have been there and I guess we all know what that is.'

As the full extent of what this meant began to dawn, Danny's whole demeanour changed and he became incredibly angry.

'The bastard, the absolute bastard. I invite him into my house and all he is interested in doing is screwing my wife. I can't believe that anyone could stoop that low. Just wait 'til I get my hands on him.

'Hang on though, how do you know he didn't commit the murder?' Danny asked.

'We don't,' replied the officer. 'But as we speak Jack is on the way to the main police headquarters in Portishead and that is where we need to take you.'

As the police car headed out of the car park, spectators and players alike were congregating in the pavilion, there followed a feeding frenzy of questions but with very few answers.

For sure something very serious had happened but nobody really had any idea that the events of that day were about to catapult the quiet village of Bundary onto the pages of the national newspapers.

The two teams separated and the players ambled into their respective dressing rooms all looking visibly shaken. Rambo addressed the Fieldhouses players with a sombre tone.

'Look, guys, I have no idea what is going on except that Jack phoned a couple of minutes ago to say that he was in a police car and on his way to the main Bristol police station in Portishead after finding Danny's wife Helen stabbed, murdered and lying in a pool of blood on the kitchen floor at her home.'

'What on earth was Jack doing at Danny's house in the middle of a cricket match?' asked one of the players.

'Well, I think you can use your own imagination to work that one out and I know that Jack had a bit of a soft spot for Helen but I had no idea he would go to such lengths to see her.'

'Well has he killed her?' someone blurted out.

'Don't be ridiculous,' Rambo replied.

'He had obviously thought that he had time to see her whilst we were batting with the house being just a couple of minutes' walk from the ground.

'I cannot believe it myself that he was so stupid to get involved to this level and it is a lousy trick to play on an opposing captain who is putting you up for the weekend. Imagine walking into the kitchen, only to find that the girl you thought you were going to make love to, lying in a pool of blood with a knife stuck in her abdomen. Look I think we need to get changed and get the hell out of here as soon as possible.'

As he finished speaking one of the police officers came into the dressing room.

'Look, chaps, I know that you are all probably as confused and upset as we are and I suggest you get home as quickly as possible before this hits the news channels. But before you leave, I need everyone's contact details so that we can get in touch with you as and when necessary.'

There was silence from Bundary's home dressing room as all the players were sat down with their heads in their hands.

The vice-captain Paul Thomas stood up to address the shell-shocked members of the team.

He had captained the side for six years before handing over the reins to Danny and had known many of the team members for most of his life. He was highly respected for all he had done for Bundary cricket club over the years and was visibly shocked as he started.

'Guys, half an hour ago we were on the verge of winning a cricket match on a beautiful Easter Saturday and looking forward to a wonderful weekend.

'Now we find out that the opposing team's captain has skulked off to shag Danny's wife, only to find her lying dead on the kitchen floor with a knife stuck in her abdomen.

'And before you ask, no we don't know whether he killed her but that does seem highly unlikely.

'I have no idea how long this affair with Helen had been going on and indeed whether they had been seeing each other or not.

'Danny and Jack are both on their way to Bristol Police Headquarters and I just hope that they are kept apart because I cannot begin to imagine what Danny is feeling right now.

'The police have told me that we are free to leave providing they can have all our contact details as they are bound to need to speak to us individually to gather information.

'I suggest that we all head off home because there doesn't seem much point in hanging around.

'It is not going to serve any purpose in trying to guess what the circumstances are behind this very sad day. No doubt it will come out in the wash as these things generally do.

'There must be much more to this than just some random murder. I doubt whether there has ever been a murder in Bundary before.'

The reporter from the local gazette was still hanging around trying to get as many details from the players as possible. But no one was in the mood for talking and certainly not to the press.

There was very little dialogue between the two teams as the players got changed, packed up their kit and headed off for their respective homes.

The police were shown Jack's bag and his belongings were packed away and transferred to the main police station.

The ladies stayed on to clear up after the wonderful banquet that was supposed to be the highlight of a wonderful day.

But as the lights were turned off in the pavilion it was to be a day that would be remembered for all the wrong reasons.

Ray Stephens hated the phone ringing at the weekend as it usually meant bad news. Through a dedicated life to police work he had risen through the ranks to Detective Chief Inspector of The Avon and Somerset Police Force and was now only six months away from a well-earned retirement and a much-deserved pension.

A tall man, with a good head of hair for his age, Ray was always immaculately dressed and although it probably wasn't true, nobody could remember him wearing anything other than a plain grey suit and a cheque shirt.

Although he didn't smoke, he looked the type that would enjoy a pipe whilst working through a murder case. He had a kind but thoughtful face that seemed to match his demeanour of composed authority.

Having encountered all sorts of criminal activity and all sorts of criminals in his life long career in the police force, nothing seemed to particularly faze him.

Joining as a "Bobby on the Beat", he had worked his way up to the top and was extremely methodical and calm in his approach to police work.

Becoming one of the youngest detectives in the criminal investigation department, otherwise known as the CID, He had earned the nickname "Mr Motivator" because of his insistence that all crimes had a motive and understanding the reason for that motive was where all good police work began.

He had worked on numerous murders throughout his illustrious career and had become emotionally immune to the variety of senseless homicides except for the murder of young children.

The unsolved case of an eleven-year-old girl, raped, murdered and left to die in dense woodland, had left an indelible scar on his memory and haunted his many nightmares.

Within a heartbeat, as soon as he picked up the phone, he recognised the voice of his sidekick Mike Salter.

They had worked together for over ten years and enjoyed an excellent relationship having solved many crimes in the Bristol area.

In many ways Mike was the opposite to Ray in that he was slim, not particularly well dressed and bit of a fidget.

He would be more of a half a fresh grapefruit and a cup of black coffee for breakfast type of guy, whereas Ray would definitely be a full English with a piece of fried bread type of guy.

He was, however, extremely diligent and had a good reputation for closing out cases.

'You don't phone me with good news at the weekend, Mike, so what's going down?' he enquired.

'Well, this is a strange one, Guv, because a young housewife has been found stabbed to death in of all places, sleepy old Bundary.

'I mean nothing ever happens there; it has one of the lowest crime rates in our region.

'Just to add some intrigue the murdered woman was found by the captain of a visiting cricket team from Wolverhampton.'

'Is he a suspect?' Ray asked.

'Well, yes, he is and he isn't but he is currently being brought to headquarters for questioning. He called in the crime and doesn't appear, on the face of it, to have a motive for killing her, but here's the bit, the murdered woman is the wife of the Bundary cricket team captain.

'The man that found her was staying at the house for the weekend.'

Pausing for breath he added.

'Boy, this is going to hit the news big-time because it is just the sort of story the press love. I can see the headline now. "Murder in the meadow of a sleepy cricket ground".'

Ray interrupted his flow.

'So, let's make sure we do everything by the book then. I want the house in Bundary secured as a crime scene and for God's sake make sure that anyone entering the property does so dressed appropriately.

'I also want the names and contact details of all the people at the cricket ground as well as all the players, umpires and any other officials. In fact, let's have contact details for everyone who was there.

'We need to shed some light on this alleged affair between him and the murdered woman.

'I think you and I had better interview the husband and this visiting cricket captain from Fieldhouses as soon as possible so I will see you down at the station at about 7.30 p.m.

'As for assembling a team, we are going to need at least a dozen people on the case so give some thought to who is available and let me know later.

'I suggest we all get together just after lunch on Sunday. Please also make sure that a fully equipped incident room is available.

'One final thing, no press release until we have all met up and understand exactly what we are dealing with.'

Mike suddenly realised that he was going to be a very busy man.

When Jack arrived at the police station, he had to undergo the usual indignities of photographs, fingerprinting, form filling and of course the removal of his cricket whites for forensic analysis.

He was handed a blanket and some clothes and got changed into the standard issue grey tracksuit that was far too small for his large frame, but when enquiring if there was a larger size, was reminded that he was in a police station and not in a posh High Street Menswear shop. He was given a passable drink of tea in a plastic cup and told that in due course two officers would be along to interview him.

As the heavy door slammed shut in his cell, he kept picturing in his mind the horrific scene of Helen lying on the kitchen floor with a knife protruding from her abdomen. He felt that at any moment he could be violently sick and suddenly a chill ran through his body as he realised that he would never see her again.

After what seemed an eternity, but was probably only an hour or so, the cell door was opened and Jack was led through to an interview room and introduced to Detective Chief Inspector Ray Stephens and Detective Inspector Mike Salter.

Ray spoke first and asked Jack if he required a solicitor and that he was happy for the proceedings to be tape recorded for further reference. The interview would also be filmed, as this was the normal procedure.

Jack immediately made the point that he didn't need a solicitor, as all he had done was discover the body of the murdered woman.

He related the whole story in detail, explaining how he had first met Helen two years ago and they had kept in touch with one another. He gave some background on the annual cricket match, which was the reason he had been staying at the house in the first place.

He insisted that there was nothing sinister in their planned meeting, other than two people who fancied each other and an opportunity to have sex.

He made no mention of the fact that they had been seeing each other on the side and that she had been selling drugs whilst working at the "Wet Whistle" pub, was pregnant or that they she was considering leaving her husband to live with him in Wolverhampton.

He assured the officers that he had no criminal record and absolutely no reason to want to murder anyone. With his background researched before the interview, he was reminded that he had been in front of the magistrate for affray.

'Oh, come on, guys, that was a misdemeanour in a nightclub years ago, what bloke hasn't been involved in some sort of fracas in their youth?'

After an hour or so of interrogation Ray and Mike decided to have a break and collect their thoughts.

Jack was taken back to his cell and offered another drink and something to eat but the thought of food was the last thing on his mind.

Ray and Mike wandered slowly into the main office.

'Unless he's lying about something, I can't see any possible motive for him to be involved in this crime,' Mike suggested.

'No, I agree, there is certainly not enough to charge him; I think he just happened to be in the wrong place at the wrong time. I can't believe he was so stupid as to remove the knife from her body, everybody knows that the murder weapon is the most incriminating piece of evidence we have to work with.

'What's also intriguing me is why the house had been ransacked?

'It sounds as if the intruder was looking for something. This wasn't just a case of opportunistic burglary in the hope of finding something of value. There's more to this than meets the eye.' Ray mused.

It was decided that given the seriousness of the crime Jack should be held overnight pending investigation and interviewed again the next day.

He was allowed to make a phone call to Rambo and explained that he was going to be held overnight so it was best that everyone in the team went home.

Rambo told Jack that all the cricket players had given contact details to the police but it was all a waste of time because nobody had a clue what was going on.

'Rambo, I will fill you in with the whole story at a later date but for now I just want you to get back to Wolverhampton and explain to my parents what has happened before they hear about it in the news. This has been the worst day of my life.'

Jack sounded completely exhausted but ensured Rambo that he had done nothing wrong except being in the wrong place at the wrong time.

He looked around the cell and suddenly realised what Danny must be going through. He would not have thought for one minute that Jack would be leaving the cricket ground to see his wife and did he have some crazy reason to be involved in the murder.

By the time Mike and Ray got round to interviewing Danny he was completely in bits.

He had woken up that morning looking forward to a cricket match and thinking that his marriage was in reasonable shape.

In less than 24 hours his wife had been brutally murdered and he had found out that she had been planning an affair with someone she hardly knew!

Danny, still in his cricket whites, was escorted to the interview room and informed that the proceedings would be filmed and taped.

He was told that this was just an exploratory meeting and that it was not an interview under caution.

As Danny was the last person to see Helen alive and also her husband, the police had more than a passing interest in interviewing him.

If he was involved in some way with the murder, it certainly wasn't apparent as he appeared totally distraught throughout the questioning and at times seemed to stare into space as though he had seen a ghost.

He told them that Jack was staying with them as captain of the visiting Fieldhouses team and that this was an annual event played over Easter weekend. He added that apart from cricket they never met for any other reason.

Ray and Mike were interested in knowing how long Jack and Helen had been having the affair and Danny explained that as far as he knew nothing had happened before the planned meeting that afternoon.

'We're intrigued to know why the house had been ransacked and what the intruder was hoping to find. Can you throw any light on that?' Ray asked.

Danny shook his head and added, 'Helen worked four nights a week at the "Wet Whistle", had very little money and certainly no possessions of any value that I know to so I cannot think of any possible thing the intruder may have been looking for.'

'What about your job, Danny? Does it involve storing any valuable items at home?' Ray suggested.

'As it happens, I do sell industrial diamonds to the jewellery trade but they are nowhere near as valuable as gemstones and I never bring them home.'

Getting mildly excited Mike proposed that it could be a very good reason for the break-in if someone didn't realise the difference in value between industrial diamonds and gemstones.

Ray was keen to get back to the relationship between Jack and Helen.

'One thing I don't understand is how Jack could leave the cricket ground, get back to the house, have sex with your wife and return to the ground, without being noticed.'

'That's simple,' Danny replied. 'Because he was the last man to be batting, there would probably be at least a couple of hours before he would be called upon. The other players would probably be watching the match or walking round the ground. It would be quite easy for him to disappear and not be missed.'

'The same logic would apply to you, would it not, Danny, you were the last man in to bat for Bundary, so you could have disappeared, committed the murder and returned to the ground without anyone missing you?' Ray suggested.

'Except that I can prove I was there for the whole innings because I can talk you through everything that happened, the fall of wickets and how people were dismissed. Ask anybody whether they saw me leave the ground and they will say no because I was there for the whole time we were batting until I went in as last man.

'In addition, what motive would I have for killing my wife? It might not have been the best marriage in the world but we rubbed along together well enough and I can't think of any reason why I would have wanted her dead.'

Danny suddenly looked a broken man and his voice started breaking up as he reached the end of his tether.

'Shouldn't you be out there trying to catch the actual murderer rather than trying to convince yourselves that it might be me?'

It was obvious that he was starting to get angry and Ray and Mike took the opportunity to calm things down by calling a break in proceedings for half an hour in order to collect their thoughts.

Back in Ray's office over what must have been a sixth cup of coffee, Mike and Ray went over everything they had been told.

'There's far more to this case than we realise,' Mike suggested.

'A young woman, who works part time in the local pub and is apparently reasonably happily married and is brutally murdered in a sleepy village, just does not make sense.

'It would appear that the would-be lover was just in the wrong place at the wrong time and the husband happened to be in the right place at the right time!'

As it was now approaching 10.00 p.m. Ray decided to bring things to a close for the evening and continue investigations the following day.

They hadn't got any reason to keep Danny in custody and he was released pending further investigation on the understanding that he was not allowed back into his house until the forensic team had finished with their investigations.

With nowhere to go, Danny phoned his parents to explain what had happened and an hour later they arrived at the police station to take him back to their home.

As he got into the back of the car he broke down in tears and related the story of how the visiting captain of Fieldhouses, who had been staying with him for the weekend, had returned to the house to find the murdered body of Helen lying on the floor.

Mike Salter was left to contact the investigation team and to pass on the welcome news that their Easter Sunday would not be a walk in the park with their loved ones but a meeting at 2.00 p.m. in the incident room at the Avon and Somerset headquarters in Portishead.

This would allow the whole of Sunday morning for the autopsy to be conducted and whilst the cause of death was fairly obvious, autopsies acted as the prism for all murder cases.

Needless to say, Stan Butcher, head of forensic pathology and post mortem examinations, was none too pleased that he would be working on Easter Sunday but as in all murder cases time was of the essence.

It was just after midnight when Mike and Ray eventually left, having agreed to meet back at the station at 10.00 a.m. the following day.

Maybe a good night's sleep would give a little clarity to what was starting to look like a very complex case.

Chapter Five

The team assembled for the Sunday afternoon meeting included Detective Chief Inspector Ray Stevens and Detective Inspector Mike Salter as the two senior members who would lead the enquiry.

The backup team consisted of Sally Marshall who was the senior crime investigation sergeant, four additional sergeants who would do most of the legwork, Bob Sheldon a young but tenacious crime psychologist seconded from the Metropolitan Force and Bob Mitchell who was Head of the Forensics Team.

In attendance was the long serving police pathologist with the unfortunate name of Doctor Stan Butcher.

Ray opened proceedings by thanking everyone for making the effort to come in at such short notice.

'As you all know, speed is of the essence in solving murders and this case is no different.

'I'm going to tell you what we know so far and then hand over to Sally as the senior crime scene investigator.'

Ray explained to the team about the annual cricket match and that Jack Reed as captain of the visiting side was staying at Danny Maguire's house over the weekend. It further transpired that Jack had arranged to return to the house during the cricket match allegedly to have sex with Danny's wife.

Not understanding the rules of cricket Sally interrupted.

'Gov, how could he disappear if he was playing in the cricket match?'

Ray explained that because he was the last man to go into bat for Fieldhouses there would be a window of at least a couple of hours before he would be needed.

Sally sort of understood but still looked a little puzzled as Ray continued.

'At exactly 4.40 p.m. the call came through from Jack that he had returned to the house only to find Helen lying on the kitchen floor in a pool of blood with a knife protruding from her abdomen.

'Now Mike and I have interviewed this Jack Reed guy, who is currently in custody, and unless he is an incredibly good actor, I think his story holds up and he just happened to be in the wrong place at the wrong time.

'I accept that it is a remarkable coincidence that he discovered the body and he could, of course, still be the perpetrator of the crime.'

Mike was quick to add a few thoughts of his own.

'It just doesn't make any sense for Jack to be the killer, what could possibly be his motive and if he was the killer, why would he call the police?

'He doesn't have a police record but he was hauled up in front of the magistrate some years ago for an incident in a nightclub and we are in the process of talking to the West Midlands Division to find out whether they have anything else on him but for the time being he has not been charged with anything but we do need to speak to him again.'

Ray wanted to make a couple of final points.

'One thing I want you all to ponder is that in exactly the same way that Jack had a two-hour window of opportunity to pop back to the house, so too did the husband Danny Maguire.

'He, also, was the last man in to bat for Bundary, so he could have slipped away from the ground, committed the murder and returned without being missed.

'He is obviously a person of interest as he was the last person to see the victim alive, and whilst he adamantly maintains that he was at the ground for the whole time, we must re-interview all his teammates to check out his alibi.

'As far as we know, he has no prior, has a completely clean record and no motive for savagely murdering his wife. And I have to stress that this was a savage attack.'

Ray made way for Sally Marshall as the senior investigating sergeant to update the team on her initial findings. She had a wealth of experience under her belt, as well as probably a few too many pizzas, but she was highly regarded by everyone in the department.

Striding confidently to the front of the room and dispensing with the usual formalities she wasted no time in getting into the swing of things.

'My first observation was the lack of forced entry and it was my initial instinct that the victim must have known the perpetrator of the crime.

'However, it is quite possible that she may have left the back door open for her planned meeting with her would be lover boy Jack Reed.'

Pausing for a sip of water whilst pictures of the crime scene were handed out, she was soon back in her stride.

'There was a distinct lack of defence wounds on her body, which again leads me to the conclusion that she knew her killer and this murder was not from a random break-in that went wrong.

'It is quite feasible that the stabbing occurred after an argument but that is Bob's area of expertise more than mine so I will try and just stick to the facts.

'The kitchen knife used in the murder was one of a set we found in the kitchen drawer and it appears that there was a single stab wound to the lower abdomen but no doubt Dr Stan will give us a full account of how the poor girl died.'

Sally took another sip of water and continued.

'There was a tremendous amount of blood on the kitchen floor when we arrived on the scene but the knife had been apparently removed by this cricketer Jack Reed and then thrown into the sink. If the cricketer is telling us the truth, then his fingerprints are going to be all over the handle of the knife and our murder weapon is going to be of little forensic value to us.'

Sally handed around some more pictures of the house that indicated that the intruder/murderer had been looking for something as most drawers both downstairs and upstairs had been opened and searched.

'I don't buy the ransacking,' she said with some authority.

'Although most of the drawers in the house had been opened, very few had been properly searched. I mean if you had murdered someone and you were looking for something I don't think you would care how much stuff was thrown on the floor.

'This was almost a tidy ransacking, if you get my drift, and I think the drawers were opened to try and throw us off the scent.'

Ray thanked Sally for her presentation and asked the pathologist Dr Stan Butcher to come forward with his report.

As if having the surname Butcher for a pathologist wasn't enough, Stan was a tall thin carcass of a man who looked as though he was close to death himself and nothing in the world would ever make him laugh. Horn-rimmed glasses adorned a prominent forehead in which, one assumed, more brains than normal existed. He looked the type who would be much happier around dead bodies than living ones and you could imagine him coldly dissecting body parts and really enjoying his work.

'Sally was quite right,' he started.

'There was a single stab wound that punctured the abdominal aorta to a depth of some twenty centimetres. With the main aorta severed, the resulting blood loss would have been immense leading to the poor girl fainting within minutes and eventually suffering a heart attack. Regarding the timeline, which as you know is extremely difficult to gauge, I would say this murder took place sometime between 2.30 p.m.–4.00p.m.

'Regarding the stabbing, the angle of the wound, from right to left, would almost certainly indicate a right-handed attacker who was fairly tall in height.'

With intonation as lifeless as the bodies he worked on Stan suddenly dropped a bombshell.

'As if the loss of one person isn't tragic enough, I have to inform you that our murdered young lady was at least eight weeks pregnant.'

There was a thunderclap of silence as the significance of what had just been said slowly began to sink in. Could this murder be associated with the pregnancy or was it just a coincidence that had nothing to do with the motive?

'Well that certainly could put another spin on the story,' Ray was quick to add.

'But before we get too far ahead of ourselves, I would like to introduce someone who may well be able to help us understand the mindset of our murderer.'

Beckoning him to come forward Ray continued, 'This is Bob Sheldon who is a qualified crime psychologist and is on secondment from the Met for the duration of this case.'

Bob looked older than his twenty-five years due to premature balding but this was balanced by a boyish smile that tended to light up his whole face.

'Good morning, everyone, and I am delighted to be working with such a professional team. It is important that we start to build the profile of our assailant from what we know. I suppose my job has many definitions but is probably best described as the study of the wills, thoughts and reactions of criminals and all that partakes in the behaviour of the mind of that person.

'As you may or may not know nine out of ten murders are committed by men as they tend to exhibit a lower level of self-control than women.'

The team listened with what seemed genuine interest as Bob continued.

'There are seven main homicide event motives of which the main ones are revenge, jealousy, hate, thrill, gain and attempted concealment of another crime.

'Women tend to murder for different reasons from men and fatal attacks by women are more likely to occur within the home environment whereas attacks by men are more likely to occur outside the home in public or other environments.'

Sensing that he may be beginning to sound a little too philosophical Bob decided to get back to the specific points of the case in hand.

'The odds are that whoever committed this crime is probably a man in his twenties or thirties and it could be extremely significant that the murdered victim was pregnant because she was stabbed so violently in her abdomen suggesting that the thrust of the knife was as much to do with killing the foetus as to with killing her. It is highly unlikely that this murder had anything to do with a break-in as there is no evidence of forced entry or defence wounds which suggests that the killer was known to our victim.'

Bob paused for a few seconds to allow the team time to digest all the facts then continued.

'Studies in America have shown that thirty percent of all murders are committed by people known to the assailant and also that knife attacks are far more likely to be reactive rather than pre-meditated.'

Sally interrupted and asked for a little clarification.

'Well, what I mean is that far more people tend to get stabbed in arguments rather than shot, particularly in Britain where there is far less ownership of guns. The fact that the murder weapon was taken from the kitchen drawer, to my mind, could prove that this crime was not pre-meditated, but it may well have been. Finally, I'm not sure whether the killer was looking for something in the house or that the drawers were opened to throw us off the scent.'

Ray thanked Bob for his thoughts and decided to try and sum up as best he could.

'OK so we have the murder of a seemingly normal twenty-three-year-old pregnant housewife whose husband may or may not be the father of the unborn child. This is a likely scenario as she was prepared to have sex that afternoon with a guy she hardly knew. Has she been putting it about with someone else?

'Sally, I want you and a couple of officers down that pub this afternoon to find out everything we can about our murdered woman and that includes possible affairs with customers. Interview the landlord, the bar staff and as many regulars as you can. We cannot rule out the possibility that this was a break-in gone wrong considering the husband traded in industrial diamonds. I want that house searched from top to bottom to find out whether there was anything of value worth stealing.

'We need to interview the husband again and find out whether he knew about the pregnancy and I want all the Bundary cricket team re-interviewed to check out his alibi to make sure that he hadn't gone missing at some time during the afternoon.

'We have four potential people of interest, the visiting cricketer, the husband, the father of the unborn child, if it is not the husband and finally a person possibly unlinked and just committing a burglary that went horribly wrong.'

Ray decided that the initial meeting had gone about as far as it could for the time being and decided to bring it to a close.

'Mike, one final thing. We need to put out a press announcement that I suggest is just the basic facts with no mention of names and at this stage the investigation is on-going and the public will be notified of any significant developments.

'Fortunately, the incident took place too late on Saturday afternoon to hit the Sunday papers but will no doubt be fully covered by all the nationals tomorrow.

'From now on this will be our official incident room and whatever you were working on before must now get side-lined until we have solved this case.

'Whilst the murder of Helen Maguire in the sleepy hamlet of Bundary did not make the front pages of the national newspapers it was certainly big news in the Bristol area. Reporters descended on the village post office, local convenience store and the "Wet Whistle" pub in an attempt to find out as much information as they needed to write a decent sized article.

'None of them really cared about the poor murdered girl or the grieving husband but it was just the sort of story that used up good column inches and sold newspapers.

'Because of the severity of the crime the police were allowed to keep Jack Reed in custody for more than the normal 24 hours. Before interviewing him again they wanted to do some research work on his background and contacted the West Midlands Police to find out if there was anything more of interest in his background.

'It was decided that nothing much more could be done on a Bank Holiday Sunday and the team would reconvene the following day.

'Down at the "Wet Whistle" pub the full-time and the parttime staff had been assembled for a meeting with Sally Marshall and two of the investigating officers, in order to get as much information as they could on the murdered woman Helen Maguire.

'It transpired that a man named Oliver Traves spent a lot of time in the pub and it was fairly obvious to all the staff that he and Helen were more than just good friends.

'They had been seen leaving together on a number of occasions although no one admitted to any knowledge of any over the counter shady drug dealing.

'A young lady called Mary Robins was one of the bar staff Helen had worked with for quite some time and they had become good friends. During the conversation with the officers, she happened to mention that Helen had suffered a period of depression due to the fact that the doctor had told her that it was unlikely she would ever be able to have children.

'Apparently, this was due to problems with her husband rather than any medical problem with herself.

'They had tried for a couple of years to have a family but after a number of tests Danny was found to be infertile.

'The detectives did not mention that when Helen was murdered, she was actually eight weeks pregnant. By all accounts Helen had been a very popular member of the team and most of the staff seemed visibly moved by the events of the previous day.

The officers thanked the staff for taking the time to talk to them on a Bank Holiday Sunday afternoon, and after gathering names and contact details, Sally phoned Mike to give him an update on the meeting and particularly the association and potential affair with this somewhat shady individual Oliver Traves.

The real blockbuster news, however, was that according to one of the barmaids, the husband could not be the father of

Helen's baby and if this was so, it put him right in the frame as a potential suspect.

The only benefit of working Bank Holiday Monday was that Ray Stephens was not working his way through typical Monday morning rush hour traffic. Just as he was approaching police headquarters his phone rang.

'Ray, this is Mike and I thought you might be interested to know that I have just come off the phone to the Bristol Police drugs division and it appears that they were watching our murdered young lady.

'Apparently as well as pulling pints of beer at "The Wet Whistle" in Bundary, she was also selling packets of drugs to a number of users and this apparently has been going on for some time.

'Our barmaid, however, is only one of a network of girls working for a major drug dealer called Oliver Traves.'

Ray pulled into Police Headquarters parked the car and continued to listen to what Mike had to say.

'But guess what?'

Mike paused to gain maximum effect.

'Sally phoned me last night to give me an update after the meeting with the staff at the "Wet Whistle" and it appears that this Oliver Traves was having an affair with our murdered victim. And if one of the barmaid's is to be believed, for medical reasons her husband Danny could not be the father of the unborn baby.

'That really does open up a whole new line of enquiry for us.'

Ray continued with more than just a hint of excitement.

'But if one drug peddler is not enough, we have just found out from the West Midlands Police Drugs Division that our would-be lover boy Jack Reed has been under surveillance for months.

'Apparently, he has been selling cocaine on the street for a couple of years. He has not been pulled in because his involvement is part of a massive drug operation code named "Operation Mainline" involving four police divisions as well as Interpol.

'I have been asked if the two senior officers in charge of "Operation Mainline" can interview this Jack Reed to try and obtain some more information on this drugs cartel and they are on the way down form the Midlands as we speak.

'Apparently, they see this as a major potential breakthrough because both Oliver Traves and Jack Reed apparently work for someone further up the chain of command, a known criminal from the Balkans with connections to an international drug ring operating in Europe.

'This would appear to be top-level stuff that has got them all really excited.'

Ray entered the incident room with a spring in his stride and a little more confidence that their enquiry was starting to take on a whole new direction.

Mike approached him to report another game changing development.

'Gov, the lads searching the victim's house have just called in to say that they have discovered a five-thousand-pound stash of money in a plastic bag in the spin-drier.'

Rubbing his hands together Ray continued.

'So, it is quite possible that the murder was something to do with a break-in at the house after all and that it just went horribly wrong.'

Mike had arranged a meeting with the boys from the West Midlands Drug Division for noon, which gave Ray time to tidy his desk and enter what details they had onto the incident room whiteboard.

It helped enormously to have all the "characters in his play", as he liked to call it, laid out in front of him. It was classic police detective procedure which had changed very little over the years.

He placed a picture of the murdered girl Helen Maguire at the top of the board drawing a line down to photographs of the first two suspects, her husband Danny Maguire and the visiting cricketer Jack Reed. A third line was drawn down to where a photograph of the suspected drug dealer Oliver Traves would be placed, once it was received from the Drugs Division.

On the left-hand side of the board Ray wrote a single word in bold italics; MOTIVE and underlined it twice for emphasis. Under this he wrote the words, revenge, jealousy, hate, thrill and gain.

The crime had to be narrowed down to its principal motive and that was first main challenge for the team.

Ray and Mike were intrigued to learn that the husband Danny could not be the father of Helen's unborn child and that she had been openly conducting an affair with Oliver Traves without any apparent attempt to keep it covered up. Under the main heading of motive on the whiteboard the name of Danny Maguire was entered next to jealousy/revenge.

They now had enough reason to get Danny back in for further questioning as he had now become a prime suspect albeit a prime suspect with an apparently rock-solid alibi.

The other main suspect was Oliver Traves, who also had possible motive and opportunity. Was Helen carrying his child? Was the money hidden away drug money that was owed to him? There were certainly enough questions that needed answers and the sooner those questions were answered the better.

As Ray continued to ponder the details he had written on the board, Mike popped his head round the corner to announce the arrival of the two officers from the West Midlands Drug Division.

After brief introductions, Joe Willets and Andy Carter proceeded to open their file notes on what had been named "Operation Mainline".

Joe was the first to speak.

'Gentleman, firstly I would like you to know that we actually work for the National Crime Agency and we are on secondment to the West Midlands Police, as the ringleader of "Operation Mainline" happens to live in Birmingham.

'As you are aware the NCA takes the lead for all investigations concerning organised crime and is the most senior law enforcement agency in the country.

'What we have here is a very complex web of cocaine distribution throughout the country that is financed with Balkan money but is ultimately controlled by a gang that originates from Serbia. We have been building up a picture of their operation for nearly twelve months now but with somewhat limited success.'

Andy broke in.

'The really clever part is how the drugs are sold through a pyramid style of distribution with four principal agents supplying maybe another ten middle men resulting in up to forty people involved in the sale and distribution.'

Ray and Mike glanced at each other with a look of bewilderment.

Mike asked how long the Drug Division had known that Helen Maguire was pushing drugs as well as pulling pints.

Andy was the first to reply.

'Oh, your local drug division have been watching her and a few others for some months now but only became aware of the sexual relationship between Helen and Oliver Traves a few weeks ago.'

Ray was keen to share what information they had with Joe and took the opportunity to break into the conversation.

'Well, what we know so far is that Helen appeared to have five thousand pounds hidden away but she was also eight weeks pregnant. We don't know whether the baby is his or the husband's or even someone else's.

'We have no idea whether the money stashed away has anything to do with the murder or just savings squirreled away. The money may even belong to the husband.

'Presumably what you guys are worried about is us getting too close to Oliver Traves and jeopardising months of surveillance.'

Joe, who appeared to be the senior officer, was the first to respond.

'Exactly that because we do not want him to become suspicious that he may be under surveillance.

'Incidentally you may also be interested to know that Jack Reed, the cricketer who discovered the body, is a dealer in the Wolverhampton area and has been under surveillance by the West Midlands Police for some time.

'As far as we know he was just what we call a part-time dealer in the sense that he was just making a few quid on the side but it was not his main source of income.

'So, we didn't feel he was a major player in the chain of command until he was spotted a couple of weeks ago having a meeting with the suspected top man and ring leader of the gang.

'For some time, we have believed that this man, named Nikolay Agapov, just maybe the top man who supplies different parts of the country through possibly four key individuals.

'We understand that one of the key suspects in your murder investigation is a man called Oliver Traves and wait for it, he is also supplied by this Nikolay Agapov.

'The coincidence that your would-be lover boy is connected to a dealer here in the Bristol area is mindboggling. It is unlikely that he knows this character Oliver Traves but it is possible that he too is implicated in some way.'

Ray realised the importance of what was being said but with some authority pointed out that he was in charge of a murder investigation that would take precedence over anything else. Finally, he reassured the detectives that he would do all in his power not to compromise their own enquiries.

Joe Willets and Andy Carter expressed their gratitude to Ray and Mike for allowing such speedy access to Jack Reed and agreed that they would not get in the way of the murder investigation.

Provided that Jack was not going to be charged with anything they had a plan, that if Jack agreed to, could help bring about the downfall of the one of the largest drug syndicates in Europe.

When the door was opened to his cell on Monday morning, Jack thought that he was at last going to be released and was wondering how he was going to get back home to Wolverhampton.

In fact, he was not about to be released at all but he was about to be interviewed by the two senior police officers in one of the largest drug cases the West Midlands Police had ever been involved with.

He didn't realise for one moment that his shady little drug business was about to be exposed and that this was about to be the second worst day of his life.

Chapter Six

At around the time the police were interviewing the staff at the "Wet Whistle" pub on Easter Sunday, Oliver Traves was hastily packing a few clothes into an overnight bag.

It was all over the news that Helen Maguire; a housewife from Bundary near Bristol had been fatally stabbed. He knew the police would interview the staff at the "Wet Whistle" pub and it was only a matter of time before they descended on him to question his whereabouts on the day of the murder.

It was time for Oliver Traves to disappear and reappear as John Roberts, which was the name on his forged second passport. He checked the photo to make sure that with a couple of days more growth on his face there would not be an identity problem at the airport. Which airport was still undecided as was the destination, but somewhere in the Balkans would probably be the favoured location.

Oliver Traves had been selling drugs in the Bristol area for over two years and had built up a network of ten distributors such as Helen Maguire.

Nikolay Agapov supplied the drugs to Oliver on a regular basis and up until now everything had operated like clockwork.

The most important part of Nikolay's job was to ensure that none of his four operatives came under any suspicion whatsoever from the police. In the event of a major problem, they had to disappear before the police got hold of them.

Two safe houses had been established, one in the New Forest in Hampshire and the other in London. Oliver had phoned Nikolay to explain his predicament and that he would be under suspicion for murder and they had arranged to meet Sunday evening at the remote farmhouse in the New Forest.

Nikolay decided to travel by train and bus to the safe house and arrived just as it was getting dark.

The detectives from operation "Mainline" had been watching the flat of Oliver Traves for some time and they phoned in to say that he was on the move with an overnight bag hastily thrown into the car.

Back at the drugs division H.Q. Joe Willets was delighted to hear that at last there was a chance that Traves might lead them to another meeting with Nikolay Agapov and allow them to understand the deeper workings of the national drug distribution network.

Up until now all communication had been conducted through encrypted text messages, which had been impossible to decipher.

If indeed Traves was going to ground for a while at another drug dealer's hideout, this was a real opportunity to shine some light on the group's activities.

'For God's sake, make sure that you are not spotted following him!' Joe barked down the phone.

'As soon as he is installed somewhere let us know and we will send some backup to surround the place. Do not under any circumstance try to arrest him yourselves. It is quite likely that guns could be involved with this type of low life.'

Joe's next call was to the Bristol CID in order to bring them up to speed with events.

He was put through to Mike Salter.

'One of your rabbits is running, Mike, but don't worry we have got him in our headlights and we will hand him over to you for questioning about the murder once we have found out who his accomplices are in the chain.'

Mike thanked Joe for the call and began to think optimistically that they may have to look no further than Oliver Traves for their murderer.

At a remote farmhouse near the New Forest in Hampshire, Oliver Traves finally came to rest. It was getting dark as he wearily got out of his beaten-up Volvo to be greeted by a somewhat worried Nikolay Agapov.

He had been born in Russia but had moved to England as he had become more important in the chain of command and the movement of drugs from one country to another.

The drugs never entered Britain through airports, arriving generally via train trips or by boat. It was Nikolay's job to vary the different routes and to find reliable mules prepared to risk their freedom for the lucrative rewards on offer.

There was never any shortage of young people, men and women, who saw no wrong in the distribution of drugs and indeed quite relished the thrill of being involved, without realising the implications of getting caught.

'So, why the necessity to disappear so quickly my friend?' Nikolay asked with his heavy Eastern European accent, as he passed Oliver a bottle of beer.

Oliver composed himself before spinning a complete set of lies.

'You may have heard on the news that a young lady from the Bristol area was stabbed to death on Saturday. Well, that lady was one of my operatives and for a while had been short changing her customers and pocketing the difference for herself.'

'So, you decided to kill her?' asked Nikolay.

Before he could answer, Nikolay put his fingers to his lips and pointed to the door.

'Keep talking,' he whispered, as he peered into the evening gloom.

'Are you sure you have not been followed?' Nikolay asked accusingly, and at the same time took out a gun from a drawer.

Peering into the failing light, Nikolay slipped out of the cottage through the back door and moving swiftly through the undergrowth soon found the car that had followed Oliver Traves all the way from Bristol.

Through his night binoculars he could see the two officers staring patiently at their phones, presumably waiting for back up to arrive.

He had seen enough to convince him that it was time to go.

He had a plan, because Nikolay always had a plan, to ensure that he stayed one step ahead of the law and that was why he had become one of the best drug distributors in Europe.

Returning swiftly to the house he bundled a few belongings into a backpack along with cash and his passport and outlined the plan to Oliver.

'My friend, just as I thought, you have been followed and very soon the cavalry will arrive, so now we go and we go quickly on foot. We will have to leave your car here, which is no big deal, as it looks pretty much worthless anyway.

'Two miles from here is the main road which is on a bus route into Fordingbridge. From there another thirty-minute bus journey takes us straight to the Salisbury train station and from there it is a regular service every hour into London and we disappear amongst eight million other people.'

Leaving the lights on in the cottage Oliver and Nikolay disappeared through the back door and into the night following a well-worn path to the edge of the forest where a wider track allowed them to move more quickly towards the main road.

They could hear the traffic in the distance and in less than half an hour of leaving, the bus stop they were looking for was in sight.

Nikolay had done his homework on the bus timetable and knew that the service ran every hour. They were in luck, as they only had to wait ten minutes before the bus came into view and they were on their way to the train station.

Back at the cottage four police cars had parked at a safe distance and eight officers had strategically surrounded the building to ensure there was no means of escape for the two men inside.

The problem was that it very quickly became obvious that were no men inside when two officers stormed through the front door and found that the birds had flown.

Just as the embarrassed officers were phoning to relay the sorry news back to H.Q., Oliver and Nikolay were boarding a train to London and planning the next stage of their disappearance.

Joe Willets, as head of "Operation Mainline" was absolutely furious when he heard that the two men had managed to outwit his officers so easily. All the surveillance work was now in jeopardy and it was quite possible that the drug distribution network would be closed down and reappear somewhere else with completely different characters involved.

He was also not looking forward to making the phone call to Ray Stephens and admitting that the chief suspect in the murder of Helen Maguire had disappeared into thin air.

He was bitterly disappointed that his officers had let the side down and the course of events had certainly not helped his own career prospects.

Ray was indeed devastated when he heard the news and put out an immediate "All points bulletin" for the apprehension and arrest of Oliver Traves. What he didn't realise was that to all intents and purpose Oliver Traves no longer existed. He had now become John Roberts and with every passing hour the stubble growth on his face was helping with the likeness on his new passport.

The search of his flat resulted in nothing of interest, as there were no clues in the form of telephone numbers or personal contact details. The flat may well have been that of the typical university student with rubbish laying everywhere and a sinkful of unwashed plates and dishes.

Interviews with neighbours shed no light on the drug dealing activities; there were no sinister midnight drops or anything to raise suspicion of any kind. Oliver Traves had led a very quiet and seemingly uneventful life, always paying his monthly rent in cash and on time, apparently a model tenant. He had now just vanished into thin air as though he had never existed.

It had been a long day that had started so well with Traves becoming the prime suspect of a murder that seemed to be connected in some way with drug distribution.

The news coverage had heightened the need for a swift arrest and prosecution, but it was now most unlikely that this would happen anytime soon.

Ray and Mike turned off the lights in the incident room and decided to head for the local pub. They always found a pint on the way home a great way to unwind and an opportunity to bounce ideas off one another.

Finding a quiet corner in the pub Ray was first to speak.

'In spite of his seemingly watertight alibi, Mike, I still think the husband is a candidate for this murder. We have to find out whether he knew that Helen was pregnant.

'If he couldn't father a child himself it is just the sort of thing that could have tipped him over the edge, let alone him being jealous of his wife going off with another man. Let's get him back in tomorrow and give him the third degree.'

Mike took the opportunity to add his own thoughts.

'We need to check out his alibi as thoroughly as we can because whilst Bundary was batting, and he was the last man to go in for the team, he would certainly have had enough time to leave the ground, commit the murder and return without being missed.

'At a cricket match people wander around the ground and do not stay in one specific place.'

Mike downed the remnants of his pint and turned to Ray.

'So we are back to the same dilemma, was this murder revenge and jealousy related or was it drug related? Anyway, I have a dinner to eat and a dog to walk so I am off home.

'Let's hope our meeting with the husband tomorrow sheds some light on exactly what did happen Saturday afternoon.'

Just as Mike and Ray went their separate ways into a cold, windy and wet evening, Nikolay and Oliver's train from Salisbury was pulling into Waterloo station.

The "Safe house" from where Nikolay had operated for two years was in Lambeth and ideally placed for travelling by train to all parts of the country

"Safe house" was somewhat of an exaggeration as the two-bedroom flat was just about big enough to swing the proverbial cat and its interior was more like a squat than a desirable residence.

Nikolay was starving and suggested a meal at a steakhouse before crashing out for the night. They both enjoyed a rib eye steak washed down with a couple of pints of beer before heading off for a good night's sleep. Over dinner Oliver began to understand the size and sophistication of the drug distribution business that Nikolay had built up.

Through his own operatives in the Bristol area, he had probably been earning somewhere in the region of £100,000 per annum. As Nikolay was earning a similar amount from four operatives, he was probably raking in about £400,000 per annum.

But it was easy money for Oliver, he was earning quadruple the national wage, paying no tax whatsoever and all he had to do was distribute the drugs to his operatives like Helen Maguire.

It had been a wonderful couple of years but now it was over and he was on the run from the police and would have to start a new life.

The sums of money involved were truly staggering, but it was all built up on a simple principle of pyramid selling and taking advantage of the massive appetite for drug consumption that existed in the UK.

The biggest single problem with the business was that all transactions had to be conducted in cash and with the money laundering rules and regulations tightening every month, it was becoming increasingly difficult to pay for everything with notes rather than bank transfers or cheques.

The New Forest cottage would now, obviously, have to be closed down but as the monthly rent had always been paid in cash with no questions asked, there was no trail of who the tenant was.

As an all-inclusive rent had been paid, including rates and electricity, the landlord would have to answer to the police why he had allowed this to happen. This was his problem and there would be absolutely no trail back to the gang's headquarters in The Balkans.

Nikolay suggested that it would make sense to get Oliver out of the country as soon as possible but they would talk about it in the morning. After a long and tiring day, they were both ready to call it a day and collapse into bed. All that was now left of Oliver's belongings were a few old clothes, a couple of thousand pounds and a new passport in the name of John Roberts.

The following morning Oliver was the first to rise and decided to take a stroll and buy a few grocery items from the local convenience store. He was also interested to see what news of the murder, if any, had hit the national papers. With it being Easter Monday everywhere was exceptionally quiet with just a few people out early taking their dogs for a walk.

Reflecting on his past, he felt that it was time to forget Oliver Traves and start to consider what a new life for John Roberts may look like working in the Balkans.

He had not enjoyed a happy childhood, as at the age of six, both his parents had been killed in a horrific car accident.

His grandparents on his mother's side had brought him up but he had never felt truly loved and had always thought that he was in the way and a bit of a nuisance.

A very average pupil; he had left school at sixteen with four "O" Levels and no idea whatsoever to do with the rest of his life.

He drifted from one job to another, without any purpose other than to make a living and started to mix with the wrong sort of people or as it turned out the right sort of people who were after drugs.

This was how his little business had started and ended up with him earning more money than he dared to dream of. His love life had also been somewhat of a car crash with relationships always seeming difficult to hold together.

Helen Maguire had been the first woman who seemed to understand him but the pregnancy and thought of bringing up a child had frightened him to death.

He wasn't ready to take on another man's wife who was incredibly possessive and emotional and it had all become too much to bear.

The police were after him now and he knew that he would be the prime suspect.

His thoughts tailed off as he thumbed through the newspaper to find any mention of the murder and was pleased to find that only a short article had been written albeit with very sketchy details.

There was no mention of any names, just bland statements that two men were helping police with their enquiries.

Upon returning to the flat he found Nikolay up and about and wandering around without any sort of purpose.

'Coffee, milk, bread and a few breakfast items,' he announced as he threw the daily paper over to Nikolay.

Nikolay was delighted to learn that there was very little coverage of the murder in the national news and pouring himself a large black coffee sat down to discuss a potential plan of action.

He did not mention the murder of Helen Maguire and seemed more interested in who could take over the drug distribution from Oliver for the Bristol area.

After some discussion a couple of names were put forward and it was agreed that Nikolay would ring the two potential candidates in the next day or two.

The remaining stash of cocaine from Oliver's flat was handed over to Nikolay with the assurance that the flat had been cleared of any incriminating evidence regarding contact names and numbers.

It was time to talk about the future in detail and Nikolay was the first to speak.

'Whilst you were out this morning, I took the opportunity to speak to my boss and we have decided is that you should move to Dubrovnik as soon as we can get you a flight.

'As you have a British passport under the name of John Roberts, you will be allowed to stay for three months without any problems.

'We have a nice little operation there with a young man who is single and about your age.

'You can stay with him for the time being and help in the distribution of drugs in the Dubrovnik area.

'He speaks perfect English, as do most of the younger people living there, and it is a fantastic place to start a new life.

'In a few months' time we can take a rain check and see how things are working out, but for the time being this is the best plan.'

Oliver had never been to Eastern Europe and was keen to learn about the region.

Nikolay was happy to give the history lesson.

'Basically, there are eleven countries that make up the Balkan Peninsula, the word Balkan originating from the Turkish word for mountains.

'The whole area was formerly known as Yugoslavia until 1992 when the countries gained independence, but not without a lot of internal strife and conflict.

'The countries you will be mostly aware of are Croatia, Bosnia and Serbia.

'Since independence, there have been many conflicts in the region with the war between Croatia and Serbia in the nineties lasting nearly five years.

'Today the countries in the region seem to tolerate each other and respect the borders that now exist but it is seen as a potential powder keg of tension that could be ignited at any moment.'

With the history lesson over, the next job was to book the cheapest flight possible from London to Dubrovnik and with several options available; a flight from Heathrow was secured for the following morning. Providing there were no problems at passport control, John Roberts would be the person leaving the country and not Oliver Traves.

The rest of the day passed without incidence as Nikolay worked his phone and Oliver seemed happy to spend his time browsing through the daily paper.

Early the following morning, with arrangements made for Oliver to be met at the airport in Dubrovnik, he climbed into a taxi heading for Heathrow, and was on his way to start a new life, with a new name in a new country.

Chapter Seven

Jack was escorted to an interview room and introduced to Detective Chief Inspector Joe Willets and Detective Inspector Andy Carter who explained to him that they were senior investigators from the West Midlands Police with specific duties attached to criminal drug distribution.

The blood started to drain from Jack's face as Joe opened a folder and numerous photographs were produced showing Jack distributing small packets of drugs to people and receiving cash in return.

Joe was first to speak.

'Look, Jack, please don't try and be clever with us in denying that you are involved in drug distribution because we have been watching you for several months now and know all about your operation.

'We have enough evidence to send you down for at least a couple of years but to be honest, we are more interested in catching the people further up the supply chain.' Andy Carter broke in and explained that together they headed up a major task force named "Operation Mainline" that involved co-operation between four police divisions in Britain and Interpol connection with Easter Europe. Andy continued, 'There are basically four main operatives distributing drugs to people like yourself. They are based in Birmingham, Bristol, Manchester and London. With each main operative supplying ten smaller fish like yourself, there are in the region of forty people involved in this gang and the numbers are growing.

'We think the main man here in Britain is a gentleman called Nikolay Agapov and with a name like that he is probably of East European descent but exactly from where we do not know. He lives in Birmingham and as you know drives a black Porsche Panamera.

'We also do not know how the drugs are brought into country and from where.

'You would have been of little interest to us until a couple of weeks ago when lo and behold you had a meeting in Birmingham with Mr Big. We have your cosy little chat in the Swan car park on film and we are very anxious to know exactly what was discussed at the meeting.'

Jack had spent his second night in custody re-evaluating his whole life. Being in a police cell had made him realise that there could be a big downside to breaking the law. Two nights was bad enough but the thought of spending a couple of years behind bars was horrendous.

He also had a pang of guilt of what it might do to his parents. He had been brought up properly in a loving home with his parents doing everything to help him along the way. If he went to prison there would be a stigma attached to the whole family.

And then this horrendous murder of a woman he hardly knew and yet had contemplated running away with when she was pregnant with possibly someone else's baby other than his. Had he lost all sense of his values?

Against this background the police could not have chosen a better moment to approach him.

'Look, guys, having spent two nights in a police cell has made me realise that it is not just a little game I have been playing which I would get away with forever. I realise now that I have been stupid beyond belief and I am prepared to do whatever it takes to make amends.

'Your timing is perfect, in as much as, at the meeting in Birmingham Nikolay offered me the job of importing the cocaine from the Balkans on a regular basis.'

He went into detail about how he would fly out to Serbia or Croatia and then travel back through Europe on the train rather than by air, bringing in four kilos of pure cocaine every trip six times a year.

'Nikolay has offered me this job and has suggested that if I accept, we should both fly out to the Balkans, so that he can introduce me to the rest of the team and the two Serbian brothers who run the whole operation.

'I cannot believe that someone I met for the first time, just a few weeks ago, would allow me to become so involved in the drug importation business, but then they ultimately have to trust someone.

'It would be an incredible opportunity for me to understand the whole chain of events, how the drugs are procured and then distributed.'

Joe and Andy couldn't believe their luck that they had found someone who was prepared to help them and work on the inside as an undercover agent.

Recognising the danger of what he would be getting into Jack was keen to get some reassurances from Joe and Andy.

'If I agree to do this and help you bring this operation down, I will obviously be taking massive risks and as with any involvement with a drug cartel, my life will be in danger. Will the slate be wiped clean as far as my previous record is concerned?'

Andy was the first to reply.

'Look, Jack, as of now, you have not been charged with anything, you have just been a person of interest that we have had under surveillance. I am sure that if you co-operate fully and help us with this case, your name will be cleared and charges will not be brought against you.

'We will brief you with all the information we have collected so far and by the way are you are aware that the main distributor for the Bristol area is the man suspected for the murder of Helen Maguire?

'He has currently disappeared into thin air and we think that Nikolay may well have engineered an escape route with the help of a forged passport.'

Jack explained how he had become emotionally involved with Helen and that he knew far more about her background than he had let on in his interview with the Bristol police. He asked if he could speak to Ray Stephens and Mike Salter again so that he could give a full account of everything he knew about her including the involvement in selling drugs and the relationship with her husband.

The meeting was brought to a close on the understanding that Jack would contact Nikolay and accept the job hoping that the planned trip to The Balkans would not be cancelled in view of what had happened over the Easter weekend. Once he had any information whatsoever, he would contact Andy immediately. Telephone numbers were exchanged on the basis that Jack would memorise Andy's number and not key it into his phone. It would not be sensible for Jack to be holding a senior drug officer's telephone number in his contact details.

Ray and Mike appeared from another part of the building and were brought up to speed with the discussions that had taken place. The atmosphere had completely changed now that Jack had agreed to work undercover for the police and close down his own little drug distribution business. It was pointed out to him that he would be dealing with very dangerous people who would think nothing of killing and disposing of him. Needless to say, he didn't fancy being the main course on the menu at some Balkan pig farm. Joe Willets and Andy Carter thanked everyone for their cooperation and headed back to the West Midlands with a real sense of achievement.

Ray and Mike were far more interested in what Jack could remember about the short time he had spent with Helen the night before the murder rather than some fanciful undercover drug operation.

A completely different Jack Reed was the first to speak.

'Look, guys, having spent two nights in a prison cell has given me time to think and I now realise that I have been completely stupid and before I wreck my life completely, I want to put things right. Firstly, I will stop using and selling drugs and as you have heard, I am prepared to work undercover to help in "Operation Mainline".

'Secondly, I will co-operate fully with your investigation into Helen's murder and do everything I can to help find the killer.

'There are things I can add to my original statement that may help you understand the background to her life. For a start she was unhappy in her marriage and had been from when I first met her two years ago, we had kept in touch with regular texts and phone calls and the occasional lunch together. Eight or so weeks ago we managed a night away in the Cotswolds together and it is possible that the baby she was carrying was mine.

'She had started selling drugs for this guy Oliver Traves whilst working at the "Wet Whistle" pub and then started an affair with him. They were planning to run away together but then she got pregnant and things started to turn sour purely and simply because she wasn't sure whether the baby was his or mine.

'In the last few months, he had become violent and hit her on several occasions. She begged me to take her back to Wolverhampton with her so that we could start a new life together.

'He would have known that Danny was playing cricket over the weekend so it is quite possible that he popped round and she tried to finish with him and things got completely out of hand. Surely the fact that this Oliver Traves guy has done a runner must make him the prime suspect.

'With regard to the husband, Danny, I can't really say that I knew him that well. Our relationship centred on cricket and that is what we tended to talk about.

'I think the marriage had gone wrong fairly early on, but Helen said that they rubbed together reasonably well considering it was a loveless marriage.'

Ray and Mike had been listening intently to what Jack had to say and obviously were interested to learn that Oliver had become violent towards Helen and that she had intended to finish with him. Mike was keen to make a point.

'Are you aware that Danny could not have been the father of the unborn child because he had a very low sperm count and that could put him in the picture regarding a jealousy motive for the murder?'

Jack reflected for a second or two before commenting that he just didn't see Danny as the murdering type. He didn't appear to have a temper or any unusual aggressive streak. As senior officer Ray thought it was time for him to make a contribution and decided to sum up as best he could.

'As things stand at the moment, as I see it, there are four potential scenarios. First and the most likely suspect is Oliver Traves, he has motive and opportunity.

'The second scenario puts the husband in the frame with a revenge and jealousy motive but if he is to be believed no opportunity as he was at the cricket ground all day. The third possibility is a burglary that went horribly wrong which has motive because of the five thousand pounds in the spin-drier and opportunity because Helen was on her own in the house.'

Jack glanced across at Ray.

'And the fourth.'

'The fourth, Jack, is that you murdered Helen Maguire.'

It was possible to cut the atmosphere with a knife as Jack realised his involvement had not been completely ruled out.

He became irritated.

'We have been through this, what possible motive could I have to murder a beautiful young woman that I hardly knew and even if I had killed her why would I have called it in?'

Mike was quick to respond.

'That is exactly what we don't know. But what we do know is that you have been in contact with each other for a couple of years now and we only have your word that nothing else was going on. You were both selling drugs so there are reasons to think your paths may have crossed. We also only have your word that you were sneaking back to the house for sex that afternoon.

'For now, though we have no reason to hold you so we shall be letting you go on the understanding that you are still a person of interest.'

Later that day, Danny Maguire was brought back in for questioning by Mike Salter and Ray Stephens. The fact that Helen was pregnant when murdered was a significant discovery in the autopsy given that Danny could not be the father.

It was made clear to Danny that he was not under caution and no charges were being brought against him and whilst he was entitled to have a solicitor present, there really was no point.

Danny stated that as he was not guilty of any crime and therefore did not need a solicitor to be present. He was offered a cup of tea before the bombshell was dropped.

Mike went straight for the jugular.

'Danny, are you aware that your wife had been peddling drugs whilst working at the "Wet Whistle" pub and are you also aware at the time of the murder, she was eight weeks pregnant?'

If he was acting, it was a brilliant piece of theatre because Danny dropped the cup of tea on the table and appeared to turn white.

'That's impossible,' he replied with apparent incredulity. 'We had been trying since we first got married to have a family, only to find out in subsequent tests, that my sperm count was too low to effect fertilisation.'

'Which proves one thing,' Ray added.

'That you cannot be the father.'

'Yes, I think I can work that out for myself,' Danny added with a somewhat angry and sarcastic tone.

Joe was anxious not to lose the opportunity of getting as much out of Danny as he could and tried to dig a little deeper.

'So come on, Danny, I know she worked in the pub and would have met a lot of guys, but you must have had an inkling that she was seeing someone. There must have been a change in her attitude towards you, not so approachable in the bedroom, that sort of thing?'

'No, seriously, I can honestly say I didn't notice any real change in her attitude towards me. She still seemed loving and caring, I never suspected for one moment that she maybe having an affair, let alone be eight weeks pregnant. I also find it hard to believe that she would be so stupid as to get involved in the sale of drugs.'

Danny seemed to be on the point of losing it completely as his bottom lip started to quiver. Joe and Ray weren't sure whether to show sympathy for his situation or take it as a wonderful opportunity to challenge him at his weakest moment.

Ray looked Danny straight in the eyes and with some sympathy in his voice started to go through the facts.

'Look, Danny, you have to understand how this looks from our point of view. With your wife pregnant by another man there is a strong motive for you to want to kill her and with you being so close to your house at the time of the murder, there is ample opportunity.'

'You are assuming that I could murder the woman I have lived with for three years and up until now have always thought I was in a loving relationship with.

'How do you know that Jack Reed isn't a raving nutcase and killed her in a fit of temper when he couldn't get his own way?

'Maybe he is involved in some way. You have to admit it is incredibly suspicious that all this happened to take place on the same weekend of a once in a year cricket match. Apart from me he was the last person to see her alive and I would have thought for that very reason he would be the prime suspect rather than her own husband.'

Danny couldn't hold it in any longer and the emotion flowed out through his tears as he completely went to bits.

Mike and Ray glanced at each other, both realising that he was either a bloody good actor or that he was blissfully unaware of what he had just learnt.

After a couple of minutes Danny managed to pull himself together.

'Look, guys, I can see why you think I may have had a motive for being angry that my wife was pregnant by another man but I can honestly tell you that I had absolutely no idea whatsoever that it was the case. And even if I had known, you honestly believe that I am some sort of psycho that is capable of sticking a knife in someone, let alone someone who I have loved and lived with for three years.

'I am a normal sort of guy who goes out to work every day to earn a living and at the weekend, during the summer months, play a bit of cricket for relaxation.

'Yes, of course, I was incredibly sad to learn that I would never be able to father a child but that wasn't exactly the end of the world for me. Lots of couples get along quite happily without ever having children.'

Looking both exasperated and exhausted he turned to Mike and Ray.

'Guys, please find the person who did this to Helen. You have to believe that I had nothing to do with this, it is inconceivable that I could be so deranged as to murder my own wife, this has to be something connected to the drugs trade that you say she was involved in.

'It has to be something to do with the five thousand pounds you found in the spin-drier.

'Yesterday, I woke up next to my wife looking forward to a cricket match and a wonderful weekend. Thirty-six hours later, I find that my wife has been murdered, that she was carrying someone else's child and was also involved in selling illegal drugs.

'I don't need a solicitor; I need a counsellor and a large bottle of brandy!'

Danny was reminded that his house was still a crime scene but he would be allowed a few items of clothing providing they were picked up in the presence of a police officer.

For the time being he was free to go but reminded to stay in the Bristol area and to surrender his passport to the local police station.

Mike and Ray retired to the canteen for a strong cup of coffee and a review of where the case was going or not. Ray was the first to speak.

'Evidence, evidence, no bloody evidence to go on. Why can't our case be more like Midsummer Murders or Inspector

Morse where there is always a pathway to the assailant? In real life it's never that easy.'

Mike reminded Ray that only seventy-two per cent of murders in the UK resulted in a conviction and that the rate of unsolved murders had worryingly doubled in the last decade. He also remembered recently reading that out of the seven hundred or so murders in the UK in 2018 two thirds of the victims had been male and that over ninety per cent of the victims were acquaintance murders where the victim and the killer were known to each other.

With a depleted task force and an ever-increasing gang culture, crimes were becoming ever more difficult to solve. It was time to pull the team together and decide a plan of action to gather as much information as they could on what actually happened during the cricket match and events leading up to the murder that afternoon.

There were a number of factors that worked in their favour, such as the number of people taking photos around the ground and videoing the match. The reporter for the local gazette had also taken numerous pictures during the day that could possibly shed some light on the comings and goings of the various team members. A swift phone call was made to the head office to ensure that all the pictures taken that day were kept secure for future investigation.

With two of the suspects now released and a third on the run, Ray suggested that a meeting of the whole team had been arranged for 10.00 a.m. the following day that Mike and he try to enjoy what bit of Easter there was left.

The meeting room was fairly full-on Tuesday morning with Ray Stephens and Mike Salter as the senior officers, Sally Marshall as the senior crime-investigating sergeant, Bob

Sheldon as the criminal psychologist and four-foot soldiers who were to do the donkeywork on the case.

Ray opened the meeting by thanking everyone for putting in the hard hours over Easter and explaining that in police work, murders, unfortunately, did not tend to happen on a Monday to Friday basis and in fact, if anything, they were more likely to happen at the weekend.

He pointed to the notice board, which had a picture of the murdered victim Helen Maguire at the top with four arrows pointing down. The names at the base of the arrows were, Oliver Traves, Danny Maguire, Jack Reed and Mr Breakin. There were then further details of each individual suspect and the relationship to the deceased.

Ray continued.

'As it stands at the moment, we have whittled our suspects down to four potential people, so let me take them in reverse order. Mr Break-in is obviously someone unknown to us that could have ransacked the house to find the money that was hidden in the spin-drier. This could have been one of Helen's clients who had found out she had hidden money away for a rainy day. But is it really likely that someone would commit murder for a few thousand pounds? Add to this no evidence of break-in or defence wounds and it would suggest that we could almost discount this option.

'We then come down to Jack Reed, the mystery cricketer from the Midlands, who by all accounts had returned to the house for a bit of afternoon nookie. Very strange that he would risk letting the side down, literally, by having sex in the middle of a cricket match with a woman he hardly knew. He could have arranged a date at any hotel between Wolverhampton and Bristol at any time. I do find his account very puzzling but nevertheless possible. The one solid piece of evidence, however, is that the murder had been committed before tea that was taken at 4.00 p.m. after Bundary had been bowled out. We know from the pathology report that the murder took place between 2.30 p.m.–4.00 p.m.

'As Jack was on the field the whole time leading up to tea, it gives him a pretty solid alibi.

'That leads us to the two main suspects, the husband Danny Maguire and the lover Oliver Traves. Oliver Traves, Helen's lover, drug dealer, no real job, dubious history, drifter, probable father of the unborn child, violent nature and who has now done a runner and disappeared into thin air. He has to be the number one suspect, or does he?

'Finally, we come to Danny Maguire who by all accounts comes across as a fairly mild-mannered type locked in a bit of a loveless marriage.

'By all accounts, and we shall check this out with his doctor, he was unable to father any children due to a low sperm count. Whether Helen knew of this when they got married three years ago, we do not know.

'But if Jack is to be believed, she had confided in him that Danny knew nothing of her pregnancy and nothing of her plan to run away with Oliver Traves. She was desperately unhappy in the marriage but when she had talked to Danny about a separation, he would have nothing to do with it.

'If he did know about her affair and her pregnancy there is a very strong motive for the murder. In the same way that Jack Reed had the opportunity to disappear for an hour or so during the match so did Danny. He could have planned the murder knowing that he would have a cast iron alibi for the whole afternoon.

'Had Jack not disappeared without being missed by his fellow players, we would never in a million years thought the same could apply to Danny.

'When we put it to him during the interview that he too could have left the field of play, committed the murder and returned to the ground, he was adamant that he could recall every detail of the innings. It keeps coming back to me that it was a strange thing to say unless he was trying to safeguard a watertight alibi.'

As Ray paused for breath Mike took the opportunity to take a straw poll of views from the team. There were one or two who thought the murder could have happened from a break-in that went wrong, but otherwise opinions on the culprit were fairly evenly split between the drug dealer Oliver Traves and the husband Danny Maguire.

Refreshed with a sip of water Ray was eager to continue.

'Anyway, it doesn't matter what we think because unless we can come up with some evidence that will stand up in court, this case is going nowhere.

'This is when the real hard police work starts. This is what we are paid to do, to build a cast iron lawsuit that we can put before the Crown Prosecution Service that will stand up to scrutiny and cross examination. As you are aware it is extremely expensive to take a case to court and the CPS has to be fairly convinced of a successful prosecution before agreeing to proceed.

'Today is Tuesday and by Thursday I want a full forensic report on the murder scene. I want DNA lifted from wherever possible, unwashed teacups, glasses that sort of thing. I want airing cupboards and wardrobes searched.

'Let's get a search warrant for the flat where Oliver Traves was living and see if we can identify his DNA from and learn anything we can from his belongings.

'Sally, I suggest you split your team so that we interview as many people as we can. We need as much information on Oliver Traves and Helen Maguire as we can get, so I suggest interviewing all the staff again from the "Wet Whistle" pub.

'Someone needs to speak to all the neighbours in the cul de sac to find out anything of interest that may have happened Saturday afternoon.

'Finally, we need as much information as possible from people who were at the ground. As Danny is a prime suspect, we need to interview every single person who was watching the match and see if we can learn anything about his movements off the pitch.

'You should spend a day going through every single photograph taken by the guy from the local gazette. He will have taken literally hundreds of photos and we can sort through them to find any of Danny or anyone who looks remotely out of place.

'Right, I think that is enough to be going on with for the time being so let's get started and try and crack this case as quickly as possible.'

Everyone drifted off in different directions, which just left Mike and Ray in the room to reflect on everything that had been said.

'So, who is your money on, Ray?' Mike asked turning to walk out of the room.

Ray thought for a while before replying in a fake Welsh accent.

'Haven't got a bloody clue, Boyo.'

Chapter Eight

Jack had finally been released from custody on the Monday afternoon but because he had travelled down to Bundary in Rambo's car, he had to make his own way back to Wolverhampton.

He was delighted to change into his normal civilian clothes but had to wait another hour before finally being transferred to Bristol Temple Meads station.

His first job was to phone Rambo and apologise for everything that had happened. Obviously, there was no mention of the West Midlands police and the connection to the drug trade. The second job was to phone his parents and explain in very broad-brush terms the circumstances surrounding the murder.

Jack felt he had been away from home for a month. Two nights in police cells were enough for anyone and he was certainly feeling the effects of very little sleep.

He kept having flashbacks of Helen lying on the floor in a pool of blood and with his anxiety levels through the roof he decided a good stiff drink was the only answer.

It certainly did the trick as he slept most of the way back and having changed trains at Birmingham he eventually arrived back in Wolverhampton.

By the time he had grabbed something to eat and made a few more phone calls he was ready for a good night's sleep in a nice warm comfortable bed.

First thing on Tuesday morning he phoned Nikolay to tell him that after a lot of thought, he had decided to accept the job offer and was prepared to start as soon as possible.

Nikolay seemed delighted that Jack was joining the team and told him that his timing was perfect as he had planned a trip to The Balkans that very week and it would be a great opportunity for them to travel together and for Jack to meet some of the team involved.

'Jack, I have a few things to sort out here in England before we can leave but by Friday, I should be good to go. You may have read in the paper about the murder of a young woman in the Bristol area over the weekend.

'Well, the main suspect just happens to be the guy who was running the whole of our operation in that region and I have had to get him out of the country as soon as possible. I just cannot take the risk of him being caught by the police and them learning about our distribution network.

'I have shipped him out to Dubrovnik on a false passport and he is going to lie low in Croatia until the dust settles over here.

'We have an operation that supplies the southern part of Croatia from Split down to Dubrovnik and he will be part of that team for the time being.'

Jack couldn't believe what he was hearing. What were the chances of the prime suspect for Helen's murder being a main distributor for Nikolay?

'So, this is the plan, Jack, I will book us both on a flight from Heathrow to Dubrovnik on Friday morning and we shall stay there overnight. We have an arrangement with a financial exchange company that will trade our English notes for Dollars, which is the currency that tends to be used in most transactions.

'We shall then hire a car and drive the two-hour journey from Dubrovnik to Kotor in Montenegro. This will then be our base for however long we choose to stay. The Gulf of Kotor has some of the most beautiful scenery on the Adriatic Coast and in the summer, it is fast becoming a Mecca for tourists to visit.

'Believe it or not, Kotor is now the third most popular destination for cruise ships in the Mediterranean after Venice and Dubrovnik.

'There are some beautiful hotels and restaurants in the region and with the modern harbour holding up to eighty yachts, it is a truly stunning location.

'But I can tell you more about the place later.

'We could not have chosen a better time to go as I have just been told that a shipment is due to arrive by yacht which is due to berth sometime on Sunday. Apparently, your background has been thoroughly checked by someone we have working for us in the police force so we know you are batting for the right side, if you get what I mean.

'You will be able to make your first trip back to England, with the goods so to speak and see how easy it is to make money and enjoy the scenery at the same time.

'As I say, I have some things to tidy up in England first, so, I suggest we talk again tomorrow and in between I will sort out the travel arrangements for Friday and where we are to meet, etc, etc.'

Within two minutes of coming off the phone to Nikolay, Jack was on the phone to Detective Inspector Andy Carter, whose number he had committed to memory without any problem at all.

With more than a hint of excitement in his voice, he explained how everything was dropping beautifully into place. Firstly, the trip to Dubrovnik and the possibility of bumping into Oliver Traves and then the short trip down the coast to Kotor in Montenegro, which appeared to be the centre of operations.

As this was a large port that could hold eighty yachts from eight metres to three hundred metres in length, Jack had been told that this was where the drugs would be brought into the country having probably travelled through the Mediterranean, The Ionian Sea and then up the Adriatic Coast to Kotor.

Jack also made the point that his involvement had to be kept totally secret as the gang had a paid informer within the police force that could make his undercover participation extremely dangerous.

Andy was beside himself and could not believe what he was hearing.

'Jack, in one day, you have potentially learnt more about this operation that we have learnt in months. We had no idea how the drugs were being brought into the country but now it all makes sense.

'The Adriatic coast is known as the Colombia of Eastern Europe as it is the traditional route for drug importers who can hide amongst hundreds of holiday yachts cruising up and down the Adriatic Sea.

'It would be impossible for customs officers to search them all.

'However, if you are off to Dubrovnik on Friday, we have to move very quickly.

'We really need to brief you on how we can communicate with each other and to furnish you with some state-of-the-art surveillance equipment.

'You are dealing with a sophisticated narcotics gang that will be very nervous about a new kid on the block and they will be watching your every movement.

'We don't have much time for training, but we have a safe house in Sutton Coldfield on the outskirts of Birmingham, that we use and I can meet you there on Thursday with a couple of my colleagues to discuss a plan of action. We have officers who are specialists in covert operations and surveillance techniques that will need to brief you on how we can obtain as much information as possible without compromising your safety.'

Arrangements were made for the meeting and Jack started to feel very excited about his new role as an undercover agent.

Back in Bristol, the murder team was working hard to collect all the information they could from their various sources.

The Volvo car that had been abandoned in the New Forest by Oliver Traves was impounded and dusted for fingerprints. His flat was checked again for anything that would lead to a DNA profile and his drawers were searched for phone numbers or addresses of his contacts.

Although he was a regular customer of the "Wet Whistle" pub, little was known of his background except that he had worked at the local primary school as a janitor come groundsman. He was known to have a quick temper with a short fuse and managed to lose his job after a disagreement with the headmistress.

The forensic team at the murder scene were still working hard and were delighted that they had managed to lift some fingerprints from two coffee cups in the kitchen sink. As yet they were unidentified but did not belong to either the murder victim Helen or the husband Danny.

House to house enquiries in the cul de sac failed to shine any light on the events of Saturday afternoon, although a neighbour did seem to think a car had been parked up for a while but had not no recollection of colour or model. Needless to say, there was no CCTV in the village that could help in any way at all.

The families who had attended the match were contacted but nothing of any significance transpired except for one man who had videoed about twenty minutes of the match. The camera was collected in the vague hope that something of interest would be found in the footage, but nobody really knew what to look for.

The cricketers were phoned but could add nothing new as they were concentrating more on the match rather than what was happening off the field.

The two cricket scorebooks were also retrieved from Alison Bunfield and Sarah Miles. They were an invaluable source of information as they gave a timeline of the game as it unfolded.

Finally, all the hundreds of pictures that were taken by the photographer from the local gazette were obtained and separated into players and visitors in the forlorn hope that something just something may turn out to be of interest. As Head of the murder investigation, Ray Stephens was sifting through the evidence on the case, or at least the lack of, it when his phone rang.

'Hi, Ray, this is Bob from forensics and I have some good news for you. After lifting the fingerprints from the flat of Oliver Traves and matching them to his abandoned car, we have now also matched them to one of the coffee cups in the sink at the murder scene.

'So, at some point on Saturday afternoon, he was there. I think you may have your man.'

Ray was beside himself.

'Bob, that is brilliant news, you have made my day. We now have motive and opportunity. If only we knew exactly where he is holed up. We have reason to believe he has fled to the Balkans on a false passport and has ended up in Dubrovnik.'

The full team meeting started at 10.00 a.m. on the dot the following morning with everyone in attendance. As Chief Inspector and in charge of the case, Ray thought it was his responsibility to open proceedings.

'OK, folks, listen up, I am going to hand over straight away to Head of Forensics Bob Mitchell as he has some breaking news.'

Bob quickly got into his stride and repeated what he had told Ray the day before. They now had proof that Oliver Traves was at the house sometime after 11.30 a.m. when Danny and Jack had left for the cricket ground.

Forensics had also discovered spots of Helen's blood on the carpet in the main bedroom, which indicated that the house had been searched after the murder.

With so many people at the party the night before, fingerprints belonging to unknown persons were everywhere and the murder weapon was of no use forensically as Jack had removed it from Helen's abdomen as she was lying on the floor.

Sally Marshall was next to speak and admitted that the house-to-house enquiries had drawn a blank other than someone thinking that a car had been parked up in the cul de sac for a while which could well have belonged to Oliver Traves.

Police officers had interviewed the cricketers and the visiting families but nothing of interest had come to light.

They did, however, have video footage and a few hundred photographs to go through over the next day or so.

Crime psychologist Bob Sheldon reiterated his belief that Helen knew the murderer, as there was no forced entry to the property or any defence wounds on her body from the attack.

He also believed that the entry position of the knife indicated an attempt to kill the foetus as well as the victim.

Ray decided to sum up as best he could.

'Look, we all know that Oliver Traves is the red-hot favourite for this crime with the husband a couple of lengths behind but we still have no proof, other than circumstantial, that we can take to the CPS.

'There is a strong motive for the husband to be involved because he may have known she was pregnant with another man's baby and also because she had told him that she was leaving. He certainly had motive but we have to prove opportunity as well.

'We must continue to sift through the video footage and photographs and see if we can spot the husband acting suspiciously but other than that we are not a lot further forward.

'With regard to Oliver Traves, we know he has motive, opportunity and a quick temper. The fact that Helen had finished with him could have tipped him over the edge but as I have said before, we have no proof.

'One fascinating consequence of this case has been our involvement with the narcotics division of the West Midlands Police and "Operation Mainline".

'Apparently, this is a case involving Interpol and other European drug agencies that have been running for some time.

'West Midlands Police had been aware of Jack Reed's involvement in drug distribution for months and this incident has given them the opportunity to offer him amnesty in exchange for help with the investigation by going undercover.

'It may well lead to the arrest of Oliver Traves but for the time we have a murder to solve and we have to concentrate on our own work. Let's keep digging and hope that something eventually comes to light.'

Just as the meeting finished at Police H.Q. in Bristol, Jack Reed pulled into the drive of the "Safe House" in Sutton Coldfield. He was met by Detective Inspector Andy Carter and introduced to two officers from the covert surveillance division of the West Midlands Police.

The details of "Operation Mainline" were explained to Jack and how Interpol was used for communication and databases to track criminals across borders. Interpol was a loose acronym for International Criminal Police Organisation and was hugely important to the law enforcement officers of different countries.

It provided a bridge that allowed individual police officers to communicate through one common contact point. With the advances in computer systems, Interpol's headquarters in

Lyons France provided a massive database of information that could be accessed by most country's police departments.

It was explained to Jack that modern surveillance equipment had come on in leaps and bounds over the last few years and that electronic eavesdropping was now possible through covert miniature microphones and radio transmitters.

He learnt that a new breed of Stingray tracking devices had been developed that mimic phone towers and send out signals that trick cell phones in the area into transmitting their locations.

This technology had now been incorporated into a normal looking mobile phone that was handed over to Jack.

Andy Carter was quick to make a point.

'Jack, it goes without saying that this phone is a very expensive and very sophisticated piece of kit but used properly will help us enormously in gathering information from the people you are in contact with.

'Criminals are very twitchy about phones, so it may well be turned off and taken away from you during a meeting, but the beauty about this phone is that it continues to operate even when turned off.

'Needless to say, we shall want it back in good working order because it would cost a fortune to replace.

'It will work with your "sim" card from your existing phone so all we need to do is change it over and you will have all your contacts from your database.'

The covert surveillance officers went to work changing over Jack's card and then produced a new bit of kit.

Handing over a small metal money clip, the youngest of the surveillance officers was first to speak.

'Jack, this is the most sophisticated money clip in the world because it doubles up as a money clip and a radio transmitter. It sends us the details of your location anywhere in the world and is accurate to within metres. If you look closely, it has a central part that is finger print sensitive and can be programmed to your specific index finger and unreadable for anyone else.

'If you keep your finger on that central point for more than five seconds it sends us a signal.

'This will be incredibly useful because it gives us a second string to our bow. Assuming the phone is taken off you it may be placed in a secure safe and a signal from it may be impossible. However, it is highly unlikely that your money clip would be taken as well, so we have a sort of belt and braces plan of action.

'We are going to suggest that you only activate the money clip transmitter if and when you know that the drugs have been delivered and you are certain of their location.

'We need to catch the criminals with the goods in their possession to have a watertight case.

'By the way, do not worry; we shall be monitoring the phone and the money clip twenty-four hours a day and we will know your every movement.'

The money clip was programmed to Jack's index finger and the phone checked to see that it was working properly before being handed over.

Andy Carter was keen to go through the plan and suggested that Jack told them everything he knew.

'Well, a couple of weeks ago I was offered the job of bringing cocaine into the country on a regular basis from somewhere in the Balkans. It now turns out that the centre of the operation is somewhere near Kotor in Montenegro and that is where the shipment is due to arrive in the next few days.

'My job is to transport four kilos of pure cocaine six times a year into the UK travelling by train through Europe as a backpacker tourist. The idea of travelling by train is to avoid the custom's hot spots and also vary the routes.

'I had no idea that I was under surveillance for my own drugs business and was about to be charged for possession and distribution with the potential of serving a couple of years in prison and a bleak future.

'It is an opportunity for me to wipe the slate clean and get my life back onto the straight and narrow.

'I am travelling out tomorrow with the boss of the UK operation Nikolay Agapov to meet the rest of the team in Montenegro but we are travelling via Dubrovnik as they have an operation that supplies the southern part of Croatia from Split down to Montenegro.

'I have no idea what quantity of drugs will be in the shipment but I know they have other operations throughout the Balkan countries as well as Croatia and Montenegro.

'It would not surprise me if we were talking about a consignment of around one hundred kilos.

'With a kilo of uncut pure cocaine having a street value of around one hundred thousand pounds, we could be talking about ten million pounds worth of drugs in total.'

Jack made no mention of the fact that he might bump into the main suspect for Helen Maguire's murder whilst in Dubrovnik as it was not really of any interest to the West Midlands Police and "Operation Mainline".

The meeting was interrupted when Nikolay called to confirm the travel arrangements for the flight to Dubrovnik.

They agreed to rendezvous at noon the following day at the Terminal 5 British Airways check-in desk at Heathrow.

Whilst on the phone Nikolay also confirmed that the shipment of goods would definitely arrive on the Sunday.

The new information meant that Andy Carter and Joe Willets would have to move quickly to liaise with the Montenegrin police force.

The head office for all police matters was in the capital city Podgorica, a two-hour drive from the coastal region of Kotor and a two-and-a-half-hour flight from London.

The head of drug enforcement in Montenegro was an ex-army colonel named Janko Kovac who fortunately spoke good English and a video call meeting was hastily arranged with him and a few team members.

Andy Carter introduced himself to the team and explained that Jack was working with the National Crime Agency and would be arriving in Kotor on Saturday with one of the drug cartel hierarchies.

"Operation Mainline" had been set up to gather information and discover how the drugs were entering the country and who were the main dealers.

The team had established that the operation was headed up by a Russian named Nikolay Agapov who was based in Birmingham and worked with four main agents who covered Manchester, Birmingham, Bristol and London.

The breakthrough in their investigation had happened when Jack Reed had been offered the job of bringing the drugs into the UK and had agreed to work as an undercover agent for the police. The reason for Jack co-operating was conveniently passed over.

Information to date was fairly sketchy except that it had come to light that the drugs were entering Montenegro on a yacht and Jack had been told that the shipment was due on Sunday and would berth in the Bay of Kotor.

At this point in time Jack had no idea who was behind the whole operation except that he had been told that two Serbian brothers who now lived in Montenegro financed it.

It was hoped that once Jack arrived in Montenegro, he might learn the name of the yacht carrying the drugs and details of where they were to be stored awaiting distribution.

Andy Carter proudly informed the Montenegrin team that Jack had been supplied with a state-of-the-art Stingray cell phone and also a money clip that doubled as a radio transmitter.

Not to be outdone Janko was quick to reply in a heavy Balkan accent.

'We only small country with just over half a million people but we have police force with more than four thousand officers and we too have latest tracking devices.

'You be interested to know that we have just taken delivery of a military specification, hi-tech, high-performance drone so that we can spy on whatever we want to.

'As you probably aware Kotor is the major gateway for drugs in Montenegro and there are several gangs who run sophisticated operations. There are also many Albanians who traffic drugs into Europe through ports around Kotor.

'If we know name of the yacht carrying the drugs, we can follow any movements without fear of detection.

'It is an incredible piece of kit that saves hours of expensive surveillance by officers on the ground and it fly at any height we like.

'The camera on board gives good picture video that we could never have dreamed of.

'Unlike normal drones we can also keep this in the air for up to twenty-four hours.'

Andy was duly impressed and admitted that whilst most police forces in the UK now used drones, he had not heard of anything as sophisticated as the one used in Montenegro.

After further discussions, it was established that a flight from Heathrow to the Montenegrin capital of Podgorica was leaving early on Saturday morning.

Janko suggested that it would be really useful for Andy and his senior officer Joe Willets to fly out and help with the planned sting operation. They did not need too much persuasion, as it was a great opportunity to get a couple of days away from the humdrum of family life.

It was not too often that the police had inside information on a potential drugs haul of this size and so much would depend on the speed of the operation and what further information Jack could gather and pass on.

He went on to explain that secrecy and speed were incredibly important as officers were known to be on the payroll of the drug gangs and sometimes months of covert operations were ruined when planned raids revealed nothing.

Marine police, harbour masters, drug enforcement officers and even politicians were all susceptible to the substantial bribes offered by organised crime gangs.

With Montenegro being a relatively poor country, it had taken years for the politicians to take drug trafficking seriously and it remained the most serious threat to the country's security.

The desire to become a member state of the European Union had prompted the politicians to tackle organised crime and corruption, as it remained a stumbling block to entry.

With a specific drug enforcement agency established and run by Janko and his team of over one hundred officers, the department had enjoyed great success, so much so that in the previous three years, thirty tons of cocaine and twenty tons of hashish had been found on transatlantic ships.

Andy and Jack could not help but admire the enthusiasm with which Janko spoke and were genuinely staggered by the size of the seizures.

Janko emphasised how important it was for Jack to establish the names of the brothers operating the cartel and if possible, where they lived and most importantly the name of the yacht and when it was due to arrive.

Jack was instructed to text as much information as possible through to Andy's phone so that a plan could be drawn up.

Janko had decided to use his own men from Podgorica for the operation, rather than risk any of the police from the Tivat province, which controlled the Kotor region. Whilst he trusted implicitly his own team, he could not risk someone from another force leaking information and blowing the complete operation.

With pleasantries exchanged and arrangements made to meet up at Podgorica airport, Janko thanked Andy for the phone call and sounded thrilled that his narcotics team would be working with a British team in a joint operation.

With the video call over it was time for Jack to get back to Wolverhampton and pack a few belongings for the early start down to Heathrow the following day.

Chapter Nine

Jack and Nikolay met up as planned at Heathrow and for once the flight was on time arriving in Dubrovnik mid-afternoon.

They were met off the plane by Macca, a slim but well-built Croatian in his mid-thirties and Oliver Traves who had flown out a few days before.

Macca was originally from Zagreb but had moved south to run Nikolay's operation from Split down to Dubrovnik.

Jack had dreaded meeting Oliver because he wasn't sure that he would be able to keep his emotions in check. Here was the man who had probably murdered the only girl Jack had ever fallen for, acting as though he hadn't got a care in the world.

Nikolay hung onto the bag full of money and passed his other one to Macca. Oliver did not offer to carry Jack's bag, which was probably just as well as they set off to find the car.

Squashed together in an old Nissan they headed off for the three-bedroom apartment that Macca rented on the outskirts of Dubrovnik. Jack was informed that he would be sleeping on a camp bed but with him being so tall he decided that the sofa would probably be a better option.

Nikolay was anxious to exchange the English notes, he had brought over, for American dollars before the bureau they used closed for the day, and they parked up and waited whilst all the money was counted and converted to dollars.

It really annoyed Nikolay that a charge of five per cent was levied but unfortunately in Montenegro, American dollars was the drug money currency used. The money was locked away in the boot of the car for safe-keeping as it was thought that no one would be too interested in stealing an old beaten-up Nissan.

After a shower and a change of clothes, they decided to walk the short distance into the city centre and soak up the atmosphere of a warm spring evening.

Dubrovnik was steeped in history, having been formed in the seventh century by refugees from Greece; it had certainly passed the test of time.

It was possible to walk along the top of the city walls and climb the perimeter towers or duck down into the evocative streets of the old town to check out the monasteries and the churches.

As they strolled through the twisting streets leading from the main Placa thoroughfare, lights came to life in the many restaurants, some of which had endured for years.

Seeing the young lovers holding hands and laughing brought all the misery back to Jack. He could have been here in a wonderful place like Dubrovnik with Helen, but that was no longer possible because in a sick twist of fate, he was about to have dinner with the person who had almost certainly murdered her.

The restaurant Macca had booked had lovely views out over the bay and they settled on an outside corner table that was very private.

It had been a long day for Nikolay and Jack and the first pint of lager went down without touching the sides.

The menu arrived and Jack was fascinated to see that "Green Stew" was a local favourite or failing that "Dirty Macaroni" which was macaroni but smothered in a rich meat and tomato sauce.

In the end he felt a bit of a wimp when he plumped for the simple grilled fish with French fries and local vegetables.

The other guys made their choices, not surprisingly nobody picked either the "Green Stew" or the "Dirty macaroni". Nikolay ordered a carafe of local red wine and a carafe of local white and they settled down to enjoy the meal.

Jack asked Oliver how he had settled in and what he planned to do from hereon in.

'Well, as you know, I had to leave England quickly because I am suspected of murdering a woman who worked for me selling drugs.'

Jack couldn't help himself.

'Well, did you murder her?'

Oliver's body seemed to drain of blood as he turned to face Jack.

'What sort of fucking question is that, you prick? What the fuck has it got to do with you? Does it matter to you whether I killed or not and anyway it's none of your fucking business!'

He slammed his knife and fork down on the table and stormed off to the toilet. Needless to say, Nikolay and Macca were not amused and told Jack that he was completely out of order to bring up the subject.

When Oliver returned Jack apologised and everything seemed to calm down as the conversation returned.

Macca was interested to know when the next supply of "Coke" would arrive as he had sold all his stock and had customers almost begging for a new delivery. Now that Oliver had joined the team to help with distribution, it was even more important to get their hands on a decent sized batch.

Nikolay explained that Jack and himself would be hiring a car the following day and driving down to Kotor to meet the rest of the team.

The shipment was due to arrive on Sunday and then Jack would be travelling back to the UK by train with four kilos of pure cocaine, which when cut with an additive would supply the four main agents with eight thousand grams of product with a street value of four hundred thousand pounds.

Nikolay would then return to Dubrovnik with a kilo, which would keep Oliver and Macca occupied for quite a while. Another four or five kilos would be distributed to other agents based in central Europe.

Over another carafe of wine Jack asked how the drug business had started up in the first place and Nikolay got quickly into his stride.

'Originally the two brothers who run the business started out in the restaurant trade. Born just outside Belgrade, they both worked in hotels until the elder brother Josif Vukovic started his own wine wholesaling business in and around Belgrade supplying hotels and restaurants with top quality product.

'He got a name for good quality and good prices and slowly built up his clientele until the business was large enough for his younger brother Dragan to join him.

'Over the next twenty years the business continued to grow and with the explosion of tourism along the Adriatic

Coast, the brothers started supplying a lot of hotels in Dubrovnik and down the coast to Kotor.

'Eventually they had made enough money to set up a vineyard of their own and bought some land in the highly sought-after region around Lake Skadar.

'Montenegro has thousands of years of wine-making tradition and is famous for growing grapes in plantations in the form of a cross. The grapes are grown either in the chalky limestone soil of the Adriatic coastal region or in the vineyards close to the city capital of Podgorica.

'The wine is produced from a wide range of grape varieties and over the last decade or so has enjoyed a surge in worldwide popularity.

'I got to know the brothers ten years ago when they offered me a job selling wine for them. I was originally born in a small town called Cherlak in Western Siberia, which is not the greatest start in life, as anyone living in Siberia is desperate to get away from it. You spend six months of the year trying to keep warm and the other six months trying to avoid mosquitoes.

'So, at the age of eighteen I left home and moved to Belgrade. For the first couple of years, I worked as a waiter in a top restaurant in the centre of Belgrade and it was there that I met Josif Vukovic who was supplying the restaurant with wine.

'He eventually offered me a job as a salesman, which I continued to do until they started up in the drug business.'

Jack was all ears at this point as he was keen to know the history behind the network and how it had evolved into the size it was today.

Nikolay downed another glass of wine and continued with his life story.

'I set up the operation here in Dubrovnik with Macca, but the big prize was always going to be starting up in the UK. There is a high demand for cocaine in Britain, particularly in the larger wealthy cities such as London, Birmingham, Manchester and Bristol.

'It has been a great place to work and learn the language because speaking Russian and Serbian doesn't get you too far in the global drugs world.

'The secret to operating in our business is never to get too greedy. There have been gangs in the past that have ended up having turf wars with each other for control of the drug trade. They inevitably end up in gun battles with many resulting deaths.

'We operate under the big-time drug radar, as the authorities tend to be after cargoes that arrive on container ships in large quantities often with value in excess of fifty million dollars.'

The more Nikolay drank, the looser his tongue seemed to get and Jack was keen to learn as much of the operation as he could without appearing to be too nosey.

Without even realising Nikolay had dropped out the names of the two brothers, Dragan and Josif Vukovic and he had also mentioned that they owned a vineyard somewhere in the region around Lake Skadar.

Knowing the surname of the brothers and the fact they owned a vineyard somewhere around Lake Skadar, would enable the Montenegrin police to identify the exact location of the operation and would almost certainly be where the drugs were stored before distribution to the other European countries.

Jack was determined to keep Nikolay talking and possibly, just possibly he might then let slip the name of the boat carrying the shipment of drugs and when it was arriving.

Macca and Oliver were having a separate conversation about the quality of the wine and Jack took the opportunity to dig a little deeper.

'So, if the brothers had such a successful wine business, why did they decide to go into the very dodgy game of drug distribution?'

Nikolay finished off yet another glass of wine but seemed quite happy to carry on talking and reveal more secrets about the brothers. He was slowly but surely filling in the blanks that Jack needed to know.

'That, my friend is a very good question and the answer has everything to do with a yacht they purchased. As the business grew Dragan and Josif could afford the luxuries that success can buy. They both purchased fast cars and spent a fortune on modernising and extending the small villa that came with the vineyard.

'But the badge of honour for most wealthy people living on the Adriatic Coast is to own a yacht and that is why the Lepo Grozde was commissioned, Lepo Grozde meaning beautiful grapes in Serbian. The yacht cost just fewer than two million Euros and was built by one of the top firms in Britain.

'However, to belong to the really elite circles of Balkan life you must be seen to own a superyacht which is usually defined as a yacht longer than forty metres. It was that desire to own a luxury superyacht that took them into the drugs trade. The brothers recognised that whilst wine production provided a good annual income, it was never going to produce the sort of return that could be made from the sale of a hundred kilos of cocaine.'

Without realising it Nikolay had walked right into the spider's web because Jack now had the names of the two brothers, the location of the vineyard and the name of the yacht on which the drugs were probably being transported.

Another carafe of wine was ordered and the conversation soon turned to drunken rubbish that was of no real interest to anyone. Jack kept repeating Vukovic, Lake Skadar and Lepo Grozde to himself and knew that if he had too much to drink the names would be forgotten.

He desperately needed to remember these names to pass onto Andy Carter and Joe Willets who were flying out the following day to meet Janko Kovac in Podgorica. The information would be vital to the drug enforcement police chief in his plan to apprehend the gang.

Eventually the last of the wine was finished off, the bill paid and it was time to return to the apartment. As Jack stood up from the table, he started to feel the effects of a long day and too much wine.

He suggested a cable car ride to the top of the city and a walk down to the apartment rather than a drunken struggle uphill which would just about finish them off. The views over the old city of Dubrovnik and out toward the Adriatic Sea were stunning in the clear night sky.

As Jack looked out over the lights of Dubrovnik, he couldn't believe what had happened to him in just a few days. This time a week ago, he was enjoying a party in Danny Maguire's house and looking forward to a future with Helen.

Now she was gone having been brutally murdered, most probably by the man he was stood next to in the cable car.

As if that wasn't enough, he was now risking his life to help uncover a major drug smuggling operation in a part of the world he had never been to.

Macca was certain he could find his way back to the apartment from the top of the city and after a few wrong turns they finally made it home.

After ensuring that the car was still outside and all in one piece, the boys crashed out and Jack settled down on the sofa.

Just as it was getting light, he checked to make sure everyone was asleep and taking the car keys from the hall table, he crept outside, opened the boot of the car, removed about ten thousand dollars from Nikolay's bag and placed the money into a plastic bin liner. The first part of his plan had been hatched.

He then texted Andy Carter with the names of the two brothers, the name of the yacht that was bringing in the drugs and the region the vineyard was located.

Andy immediately forwarded the details onto Janko at police headquarters in Podgorica.

Back at police headquarters in Bristol, Ray Stephens, Mike Salter and the team had been feeling sorry for themselves, as there had been no further developments in the murder enquiry, no further development that was until Friday morning when out of the blue, senior crime investigator Sally Marshall received a phone call.

Mary Robins, a barmaid at the "Wet Whistle" pub had spoken to Sally when the staff was interviewed the day after the murder.

She explained that over the last year or so, she had become good friends with Helen and that there was far more to the murder than the police realised and she had some information that could be really important.

A meeting was arranged for Friday lunchtime at the police station so that Mary could meet up with some of the team and tell them what was on her mind.

The team listened intently as Mary explained that she knew that Helen was working for Oliver Traves and selling drugs to some of the customers at the "Wet Whistle" pub, but that wasn't all she was doing.

They had been invited by two businessmen, who were up from London, to escort them for the evening and earn some money on the side. They were paid two hundred and fifty pounds each and enjoyed a thoroughly good night.

This proved to be the start of a business they then set up on the Internet which they named "Charm on your arm". It turned out that there was a huge demand from businessmen staying overnight in Bristol that could have some fun on company expenses.

Although Helen was married, Danny worked all over the country selling his industrial diamonds and was sometimes away two or three nights a week. Mary was single so had no ties and between them they started to build up quite a nice little side-line.

For a few months all went well and the girls enjoyed some good nights out and also earned some extra money on the side but as with most escort work, it was fraught with danger.

One of Helen's regular clients wasn't a businessman from London but a restaurant owner called Paul who came from

Portishead. Mary couldn't remember his surname but thought that the name of the bistro was something like "La Traviato".

Sally chose a moment to break in.

'So, Helen in effect was trying to keep three plates spinning at the same time; firstly, her husband Danny, secondly her boyfriend Oliver Traves and thirdly this bistro owner called Paul. Sounds quite a girl.'

Mary was quick to jump to Helen's defence.

'Well, yes, I understand how it looks but the affair with Oliver Traves only happened because she was desperately unhappy with Danny. Effectively they lived separate lives. He worked away from home a lot and then during the summer months he spent most of his leisure time down at the cricket club.

'When she found out that Danny's sperm count was too low for them to have children, it effectively finished the marriage and Helen was looking for a way out.

'The relationship with Oliver seemed to work well because he was a bit of a loner but things changed when this Paul bloke came on the scene.

'He was married with three young daughters and effectively paying to go out with Helen and presumably having sex with her. Needless to say, Oliver eventually found out what was going on and then it got really nasty.

'One night he followed them to a hotel and all hell broke loose when he kicked the bedroom door open and caught them in the act. He made sure it was captured on his phone.

'Paul ended up with a bloody nose but worse was to follow when Oliver saw it as a wonderful opportunity for blackmail and demanded five thousand pounds for his silence.'

Mike, who had been listening intently, made the point that these five thousand pounds could well have been the money found in the spin dryer.

Mary continued.

'Well, now we come to the really interesting bit, because Helen had told me that Oliver had agreed with Paul that the money would be delivered to Helen's house on Easter Saturday and in return for the money, he would delete the video he had taken.

'Oliver knew that Danny was playing an important cricket match and that he would be out of the house before lunchtime.

'Is it possible that Paul delivered the money and a fight broke out?

'Is it possible that Paul took a kitchen knife to Oliver and Helen got stabbed trying to come between them?'

You could have heard a pin drop as everyone in the room looked at each other as they realised that Helen could have been murdered by accident.

The incredibly frustrating fact was that when Jack discovered Helen lying in a pool of blood on the kitchen floor, he instinctively removed the knife not realising that he was also contaminating any potential fingerprints.

Ray couldn't believe what he had just heard and thanked Mary for taking time out to fill them in with so much information.

He suggested to her that "Charm on your arm" might not be the best career move for a single girl and wished her all the best for the future.

With Mary gone, Ray was the first to speak.

'Right, so now we know that there is one more potential suspect and we also possibly know why there was five thousand pounds in the house.

'We had better find this chap Paul who owns a bistro in Portishead called La Triviato or something similar and get him in for questioning. This case has just been blown wide open.'

Chapter Ten

Jack was woken on Saturday by the early morning shafts of light pouring through the blinds of the apartment onto his eyes.

He blinked and his stomach turned over as he thought about the enormity of the day ahead.

He had no training in undercover police work, yet here he was, in a foreign country, helping the national crime squad in a multi-million-dollar drugs operation that could well cost him his life.

It was too late to back out now and the first thing he had to do before the others woke up was to text Andy Carter again with the information, he had gleaned from Nikolay the night before at the restaurant.

He felt like he could be signing his own death warrant as he typed out the following onto his phone.

... Dragan and Josif Vukovic owners of a vineyard near Lake Skader, goods arriving Sunday on the Lepo Grozde into The Bay of Kotor.

Having checked three times that the text had been sent; he deleted it and immediately felt that the weight of the axe on the back of his neck had been lifted.

The next part of his plan was to plant the ten thousand dollars he had removed from the boot of the car under Oliver's mattress. This somewhat depended on Oliver taking a shower before breakfast and Jack being able to move the plastic bag from the sofa to his bedroom without being seen.

Nikolay was the first to rise and after taking a shower wandered into the kitchen.

Slowly but surely, everyone came round and gravitated towards the kettle and a cup of hot coffee.

Jack noticed Oliver heading for the bathroom and whilst Macca and Nikolay were talking in the kitchen, he sneaked into Oliver's bedroom and spread the ten thousand dollars evenly under his mattress.

After everyone had showered and eaten a very basic breakfast, Macca drove Jack and Nikolay down to the car rental company and after filling in a few forms they were on their way to Kotor.

It was a beautiful sunny morning and the scenery along the coast road was stunning with views over the Adriatic Sea to the west and beautiful mountains to the east.

Nikolay's driving left a lot to be desired but the road was fairly straight and the traffic was light. As they approached the border for Montenegro, a short queue had built up and Jack took the opportunity to spring the next part of his plan.

Having been asked whether he had slept well on the sofa, Jack mentioned that the only time he had woken was when Oliver had gone outside at sometime during the night, presumably to get some fresh air.

He didn't labour the point but at least now he had sown the seeds of blame for when Nikolay would open his bag of money to realise it was ten thousand dollars light.

After driving through a maze of narrow and winding lanes they arrived in the old walled city of Kotor exactly two hours after leaving Dubrovnik.

Bordered by towering limestone cliffs Nikolay was keen to show Jack some of the beautiful churches and palaces that had been built by the many wealthy families that had inhabited Kotor between the fifteenth and eighteenth century.

They stopped for a drink at the famous Letrika bar, which was one of the main hangout spots for the locals.

Jack couldn't help noticing the number of stray cats that were wandering around the town and learnt that the cat is a symbol of good luck for Montenegrins. Apparently so many ships visited the Bay of Kotor that when the sailors came home, they brought the cats with them. Because the ships travelled all around the world the feline population became as diverse as it was extensive.

The mountainous entrance to the Bay of Kotor framed a truly beautiful view of the surroundings with the deep fjord allowing passage to even the largest cruise ships.

Nikolay was anxious to move on and show Jack the real jewel in the crown of Kotor, the recently developed Porto Montenegro.

Originally transformed from a historic naval base in the deep fjord of Boka Bay, Porto Montenegro had grown into one of the top luxury yacht marinas in the world.

With four hundred and fifty berths, taking in super yachts up to two hundred and fifty metres in length, it compared to other major Mediterranean ports such as St Jean-Cap-Ferrat in the south of France or Puerto Banus in Marbella, Spain.

Just over a decade old, it now boasted palm-tree lined boulevards with high-end stores and any number of cafes and restaurants.

With Tivat airport being a twenty-minute drive away, this part of the Balkans was set to become a tourist attraction of great potential in the coming years.

Nikolay took Jack into the prestigious five-star Regent Hotel complex for some lunch and as they gazed out at the luxury yachts and the beautiful scenery, he couldn't think there was a better place anyone could wish to be.

There seemed to be any amount of fifty metre yachts costing upwards of fifty million dollars and he wondered how many people in the world could afford to own such incredibly expensive trophies.

The vineyard owned by the Vukovic brothers was close to Virpazar, a picturesque village near Lake Skadar, roughly an hour's drive from Porto Montenegro.

Nikolay suggested that they make tracks, as they were expected at the villa sometime mid-afternoon and he didn't want to risk arriving late.

Jack's stomach turned over once again as he realised this was no holiday jaunt to stay in a vineyard, but a trip to somewhere that might just end up as his resting place.

Apparently the two brothers were looking forward to meeting Jack and a meal at the vineyard had been planned for the Saturday night. Nikolay was excited to be back in Montenegro and meeting up again with the rest of the team.

If all went to plan the drugs would arrive the following day and they would have at least six month's supply to satisfy demand.

As Nikolay chatted away, Jack checked that he still had his mobile phone on him and that the money clip was still there in his back pocket. He also noticed that his heart was beating somewhat faster than normal.

There was no grand entrance or sign to the vineyard but a narrow track of approximately three kilometres led up to a walled entrance with two imposing electric gates.

Nikolay spoke into the video intercom control and the giant gates swung open to reveal rows upon rows of vines that disappeared into the distance.

He explained that the whole site covered just under a square mile, contained two natural lakes and was surrounded by mature trees that seemed to attract an abundance of wildlife.

The trees and lakes had been there for hundreds of years and over time families of birds returned to the same nesting sites year after year.

The villa came into sight, and whilst not huge, it boasted a certain rustic grandeur with a very distinctive patio overlooking one of the lakes. To the rear of the villa there were two very ordinary looking buildings, which presumably housed all the wine producing equipment.

As they pulled up at the entrance a maid appeared from nowhere to help with their bags and showed them to their rooms. Needless to say, Nikolay took care of the bag that contained all the money.

They were told that drinks would be served on the patio at 6.00 p.m. Jack was informed that due to the location of the villa there was no mobile telephone signal and that any calls would have to be made on the landline in the main house.

As Jack was worrying how he was now going to contact Andy Carter, there was a knock at his door and a furious Nikolay burst into his room.

'You are not going to believe this, Jack, but that low-life bastard Oliver Traves has stolen ten thousand dollars of the money I exchanged in Dubrovnik.

'I cannot believe he was so stupid as to think he would get away with it. You mentioned that you had heard him get up in the middle of the night to get some fresh air. He must have opened the boot of the car and taken the money out whilst we were all asleep.

'I help him to get out of the country when he is wanted for questioning by the police for murder, give him a new passport and identity and this is how he thanks me.

'Right, I need to call Macca to sort this out.'

Jack was delighted that his plan had worked and wondered what would happen when Macca found the money hidden under Oliver's mattress. He was, however, far more concerned that his phone was not operating at all and that he had no means of communication with the outside world.

As he was leaving his room for drinks on the patio, a very happy looking Janko Kovac was greeting Joe Willets and Andy Carter at Podgorica airport.

He could hardly wait to pass on the good news.

'Gentlemen, thanks to your undercover informer, we have managed to find out many things about the Vukovic brothers. We have established where vineyard is near Lake Skadar and more important we know that their yacht the Lepo Grozde is at moment in small marina in south of Albania.

'Harbour master in Porto Montenegro tell us that the yacht left on Wednesday to travel to Orikum yacht marina in the southern part of Albania. Yacht booked to return to Kotor Porto Montenegro on Sunday afternoon.

'We think we know how drugs being moved.

'We think ship arrived in Durres, which is the largest port in Albania, sometime last week with drugs on board. As there are no facilities for yachts in Durres, drugs moved by car to Orikum, which is only two-hour drive south. Once there, drugs hidden in Lepo Grozde and transported back to Porto Montenegro leaving early tomorrow, arriving mid-afternoon.

'We do not know how drugs will be moved from yacht to the vineyard in Virpazar.

'We very lucky that vineyard is only thirty kilometres or thirty minutes from Podgorica.

'We already have eyes watching yacht in Orikum and tomorrow our wonderful drone will be following journey all way back to the bay of Kotor and we can see where, when and how the drugs moved from yacht.'

Both Joe and Andy were highly impressed at the speed with which Janko had put all the intelligence together and thanked him for all his work. A private room at a local restaurant had been booked for the evening so that all the plans for the following day could be talked through.

Having booked in at their hotel, Andy checked his phone again and was worried that he had heard nothing from Jack and wondered how on earth the plan was going to play out the following day.

Jack wandered onto the balcony at exactly 6.00 p.m. and was introduced by Nikolay to the members of the family, the two Vukovic brothers, the vineyard manager Vlado Petrovic and the head of finance Spridon Ilic.

The brothers were well tanned with deep-set eyes that appeared more threatening than welcoming. They were not particularly tall but were well built with muscular looking forearms and large hands.

The vineyard manager was ridiculously thin but wiry and looked as though he lived on a diet of grapes and nerves.

The head of finance chewed on a fat cigar, was somewhat overweight, but spoke with the assurance of someone who had made a lot of money.

Nikolay was keen to explain to everyone that Oliver Traves had stolen ten thousand dollars from the group whilst they were in Dubrovnik. He had tried to make a run for it but Macca had shot him as he tried to escape.

The brothers, who spoke broken English, didn't seem unduly bothered about the incident, as Josif asked Nikolay if he had disposed of the body in the normal way. Nikolay nodded.

Josif continued.

'You see, Jack, when you live in a country where drugs are trafficked, people will kill each other without a second thought. People disappear here all the time and then no body, no crime.

'Let me explain, you see, we have a friendly man called Banjo who lives on his own, very quiet, keeps very much to himself and owns a small farm in the countryside between Dubrovnik and Kotor.

'He keeps chickens, a few sheep and some very hungry pigs. He does his own slaughtering so a few years ago we bought him a nice top of range bandsaw that cut up all things into very nice pieces so pigs can eat without indigestion.'

There was a cackle of laughter from the others as Josif continued.

'So, he very happy that from time to time we bring him some food for his little piggies. He asked no questions, we tell no lies, everybody happy.'

As the last of the roosting birds fought for space on the lakeside trees in a cacophony of chaos, and the sun slowly fell from the sky, Jack couldn't help but feel that the conversation didn't exactly fit the mood of the evening.

As the six of them moved through to the dining room, he realised that in this part of the world, life was cheap and to survive you had to live on your wits.

As if the gruesome disappearance of Oliver Traves wasn't bad enough, the main course was brought in for all to see, a six-week-old suckling pig complete with an apple in its mouth.

Whatever appetite Jack had built up, vanished in a second as his stomach once again knotted up.

As the wine glasses were filled Nikolay recounted the story of how Jack had been selling drugs back in England for a couple of years and had accepted the job to ferry them from Montenegro back to England. He had no police record, was single and ambitious enough to take the necessary risks.

The younger brother Dragan spoke for the first time.

'Jack, you are welcomed into the Vukovic family, we have done our homework on you and if you look after us, we will look after you.

'Our operation very different to big drug gangs.

'Big drug gangs try to bring in cocaine by the tonne into the country and police have to do something.

'The gangs fall out with each other; they kill each other to try to gain control.

'We small time operators in comparison.

'Since Albania opened up in the 1990s there has also been mass cannabis production and it is now out of control.

'In 2016 the police destroyed 2.5 million cannabis plants.

'But as fast as they cleared one area, another one opened up. The gangs can operate easily up in the mountains between Albania and Montenegro.

'So, the police spend most of their time trying to catch Albanian drug lords.

'So, our little operation flies under the radar of big police searches.

'It probably better for our finance man Spiridon to explain how our little operation came into being and how we continue to make it work.'

Spiridon was clearly very bright and spoke perfect English as he had worked in America for five years. He was keen to tell the story of how the brothers had become involved in the drug distribution business.

'Our wine wholesaling business had grown over twenty years to become one of the largest along the Adriatic Coast and eventually we were able to buy this wonderful vineyard here in Virpazar.

'We decided to grow two grape varieties, Chardonnay and Merlot along with Vranac, which is unique to the Dalmatian Coast. We sell mostly to the wine co-operatives and because of that it is a very simple business but also, in some years, not particularly profitable.

'We were thinking of other business opportunities and one night we had a brainwave.

'A big friend of Josif's owned a furniture wholesaling business in Tirana, the capital of Albania. Since independence, his business had grown substantially and he was importing goods from South America and then selling on to other wholesalers in Europe.

'Sourcing cocaine in South America was as easy as buying bananas, the difficult bit was how to transport them back to Montenegro.

'I flew to Colombia and negotiated a deal with a small furniture making company just outside the city that specialised in making coffee tables and cupboards from the highly sought-after Spanish cedar wood.

'We would buy two shipments a year and the cocaine would be hidden in false bottoms in the cupboards. They never asked questions about why the false bottoms were needed but it was fairly obvious.

'Cocaine production in Colombia is a way of life and forms a major part of the economy. There are any number of cartels that exist and fierce competition between them ensures that loyalty and secrecy are of paramount importance to survival in the murky world of drug dealing. Buying the drugs, therefore, at the best possible price is not a problem.

'The clever part is the distribution. The goods are moved by road through the centre of Brazil via Manaus on a journey of over a thousand miles to the Port of Belem on the east coast of South America.

'The drugs are then shipped across the Atlantic to the Port of Agadir in Morocco. From there it is a journey up to the Straits of Gibraltar, through the Mediterranean into the Adriatic Sea and finally into Durres, the largest port in Albania.

'Albania has been chosen as the final entry port of entry because the chief customs officer was bought out of poverty, shall we say, by turning a blind eye to the twice-yearly cargo of furniture from Belem.

'Once delivered to the furniture warehouse in Tirana, the drugs are collected and transported south by road to the quiet Orikum marina.

'Needless to say, the furniture wholesaler in Tirana pays very little for the goods but at least all the paperwork is completely legitimate for any customs inspection.

'And tomorrow, hopefully, the journey ends when at first light the Lepo Grozde will sail up through the Cape of Rodon, into the Adriatic Sea and finally come to rest in the Bay of Kotor.

'From beginning to end it takes ten weeks to move the valuable cargo from Colombia to Montenegro and expensive freight charges into the bargain. Nevertheless, the cost of the cocaine, furniture, transport and all the other expenses, comes to a small percentage of the street value of one hundred kilos of pure cocaine.

'We have been running this operation for three years now with not a single problem. As I said before the secret is not to be too greedy. We can hide one hundred kilos of cocaine quite easily into the furniture.

'If you can imagine one hundred bags of sugar, it does not take up a great deal of space with twenty bags secured into five false bottoms in the cupboards, which in turn is only a very small part of the container load, which in turn is only one container from a shipload of maybe five hundred to a thousand.

'Most of drug shipments that get seized are the result of tip offs to custom officers. Quite often a rival gang will inform the authorities about a shipment en route somewhere. It keeps the supply levels down and in turn keeps the price levels up, having said that so much cocaine is getting into Europe that the price if anything is coming down.

'We have all seen programmes on television of border control officers at airports seizing drugs that individuals try to take into a country. But it is a risk and reward business as it is estimated that ninety-five per cent of all drugs get through customs unnoticed.

'The success rate of drugs getting through custom controls at sea ports is even greater particularly if you use obscure ports such as Agadir and Durres.'

Josif had been quietly drinking at least twice as much as everyone else and appeared delighted that the local Vranac wine had gone down so wonderfully well with the suckling pig, he looked as though he was in seventh heaven as he too lit up a great fat cigar.

The thin, wiry vineyard manager Vlado Petrovic looked as nervous as a kitten as he struggled to get through his meal. It was obvious that he spoke very little English and had probably only been invited to make up the numbers and give him a bit of a treat. In contrast to Josif, he had hardly touched his first glass of wine and the poor chap really did look completely out of his depth.

Jack was desperate to appear interested in the supply chain and asked Spiridon how the prices of purchasing cocaine varied in the South American countries.

'That, Jack, depends on whether you want to risk dealing with a gang that may take your money and then kill you or pay more and live a little longer. We could buy cocaine for eighteen hundred dollars a kilo but we actually pay two thousand dollars a kilo because the extra two hundred dollars at least buys us some security.

'The most dangerous part of the whole business is the amount of cash that has to be carried around. I take two hundred and fifty thousand dollars with me when I fly to Colombia.

'It is not as though I can pay for the drugs by international BACS transfer and as you can imagine I cannot feel safe carrying that amount of money around in Colombia, so I am never happier than when I have paid for the goods and they are on the way back to Albania.

'Again, not being too greedy, I never have to visit Colombia more than twice a year and we have a legitimate import business of the furniture that makes sense for me to be in the country. Customs officers are naturally very suspicious of anyone making regular trips to Colombia, Bolivia or Peru.'

Appearing from behind a cloud of smoke coming from his cigar Josif was keen to make a point.

'As you have seen over this weekend, Jack, the biggest problem with drug industry is that it is all about cash. First of all, Nikolay has to change British pound notes into American dollars in Dubrovnik, because that is the currency of the drug world. We need that money tomorrow in dollars to pay the captain of the Lepo Grozde who has travelled with the goods from Colombia.

'That has cost us five per cent in exchange costs, but it has also cost a greedy young man his life. If cash is lying around the temptation to steal is automatically bigger.

'Nowadays, banks want to know where money come from. Very difficult to pay in large amounts of cash without questions being asked. Maybe also very dangerous for you to keep money in your house in England.

'In England, money is British Pound, in most of Europe it is the Euro, in Serbia is the Dinar, in Hungary it is the Forint and so on.

'Spiridon work very hard to build up good relation with banks and we move money around so it is difficult to track. Banking the money is more difficult than transporting the drugs from Colombia.

'Fortunately, we still have wholesale wine business throughout the Balkans, so we can generate bogus invoices and claim that they are paid in local currencies. This allows us to pay in those local currencies into our bank with legitimate reason.

'A lot of those super yachts you see in Porto Montenegro have been bought with dirty money.

'These yachts can cost twenty, thirty million dollars so it is one way to get rid of cash.

'If you no like boats maybe the answer, is we all bathe in it instead of spending it.'

Everyone laughed as Spiridon disappeared behind yet another cloud of smoke.

Jack couldn't help but be impressed by the sheer scale of the operation and as another glass of wine went down, the knot in his stomach slowly started to loosen. He realised that the following day could see the end of this wonderful, but nevertheless highly illegal business, and the Vukovic brothers could be in handcuffs and off to the cells in Podgorica.

He couldn't believe that just on the word of Nikolay they had allowed a complete stranger into knowing the finer details of their operation. Why would they trust him with so much information whilst hardly knowing him, or at least getting him to prove his loyalty over a period of time?

He could only think that because everything had gone so smoothly for three years that they were becoming lazy with security. Oliver Traves had lost his life for stealing ten thousand pounds from them, or so they thought, but they were right on the cusp of losing their liberty all because they had trusted a total stranger.

It just did not make any sense at all.

The brothers could see that the poor old vineyard manager was struggling with the conversation and decided to bring the evening to a close. The suckling pig had not died in vain and there were too many empty wine bottles scattered around the table to count.

Josif rose to his feet as if he was about to make a grand speech.

'Gentlemen, a truly wonderful evening and tomorrow, God willing, we receive our little parcels and we can start distribution to our important customers throughout Europe.

'Now it is time to sleep, so "Ziveli" and good night.'

As they staggered off to their respective rooms, little did any of them know that just thirty kilometres away in a small restaurant in Podgorica, the downfall of the Vukovic drug empire was being plotted.

Having also enjoyed a local meal and some fine Montenegrin wine, Joe Willets, Andy Carter and Janko Kovic were pouring over a map of the Balkans when Janko's phone rang.

'Sir, you will be delighted to know that the drone is in place, hovering on a cool evening sea breeze, three thousand feet above the Lepo Grozde in Orikum and ready to follow the yacht as soon as it sets sail.'

Janko was on fine form and patently excited about the forthcoming day.

'Excellent, excellent, now we can watch every single minute of the journey from Orikum to the Bay of Kotor and follow the drugs when they are removed from the boat and hopefully that will be straight to the vineyard.

'Tomorrow we must plan how much back up we shall need, close off all escape routes, ensure the safety of your man Jack Reed and above all ensure that we catch the brothers red-handed with the drugs in their possession.'

Joe Willets was quick to add that although Jack couldn't use the phone, as there was no mobile signal, they knew he was situated at the vineyard because it still sent out a pulse that indicated its location to within metres.

The police officers also decided to call it a day, as there was little else that could be done that night.

As secrecy was the key to the operation, they were also anxious not to mobilise too many men too early, in case anyone was on the payroll of the brothers and could warn them of the planned sting.

As Jack lay in his bed, his thoughts returned to exactly a week before when he was lying in a police cell in Portishead after finding the brutally murdered body of a young woman whose life had been so tragically cut short.

Chapter Eleven

The name of the bistro in Portishead was actually "La Traviato" and owned by a man called Paul Mason.

When Detective Inspector Mike Salter eventually tracked him down, he pretended not to know anyone called Helen Maguire.

But when Mike gave him the opportunity to be interviewed either at the restaurant, his home or at police headquarters, he changed his tune quickly and agreed that as the police station was not far from where he lived, he would attend a meeting on Sunday morning.

As he was introduced to Ray Stephens, Mike Salter and Sally Marshall, it was explained to him that the three of them were the lead team investigating the violent murder of Helen Maguire at her home in Bundary on the afternoon of Easter Saturday.

Ray was first to speak and immediately went on the attack.

'Paul, a week ago yesterday a beautiful young woman was fatally stabbed and please do not insult us by trying to say that you didn't know who she was.

'We know for certain that you were seeing her and have been for quite some time now. You are also acquainted with her friend and business associate Mary Robins.

'We would like to understand the relationship you had with Mrs Maguire and also your movements for last Saturday afternoon.'

Paul remained quite calm and recounted how he had first met Helen through the "Charm on Your Arm" escort agency and it had a sparked a relationship between them.

Sally Marshall couldn't help herself and dived straight in with an obvious question.

'So, what makes a married man, with three daughters and a successful business decide to pay for escort services that could lead him into trouble?'

Paul went straight on the defensive and pointed out to Sally that what he chose to do in his private life was nothing to do with her, not against any law that he knew off and quite frankly none of her business.

'It is my business if that association leads to, or has any connection to the murder Mr Mason. I can and will ask any questions that I think are relevant to the case, and just for clarity what were your movements a week last Saturday lunchtime just so that we can rule you out of our enquiries?'

Hesitating for just long enough to interest Ray Stephens that he looked slightly uncomfortable, he began his reply.

'I can remember exactly what I was doing, because I needed a few things for the restaurant which I could get at the Mall at Cribbs Causeway. I left home about noon, I was there for about an hour, maybe an hour and a half, and then drove straight home.'

Ray calmly leaned across the table and with a map in his hand pointed to the M5.

'So, Paul, you are telling us that you left home, joined the M5 at junction 17 and drove to the exit for Cribbs Causeway at junction 19, returning exactly the same way about an hour later. No deviations, no McDonalds on the way home or anything?'

'Yep, that's about it. Nothing more exciting than that,' Paul replied with some authority.

Ray called a break for and pulled Mike to one side near the window to the car park.

'Mike, assuming that is his car outside, just go and check with traffic and ask them to key in the number plate to see whether that car turned off the motorway on the way back to Portishead onto the A4 towards Bundary between say 1.00 p.m. and 2.00 p.m. on Easter Saturday.'

With vehicle number plate recognition standard on motorways, within twenty minutes, traffic had identified Paul's car travelling south on the M5 and low and behold, he did turn onto the A4 towards Bundary at around 1.15 p.m. on Easter Saturday.

The team had kept Paul sweating for about thirty minutes, when Mike came into the room and handed Ray the photographic information from traffic.

Ray pounced like a cat on a mouse.

'Paul, why are you lying to us about your movements on Easter Saturday? If you drove straight home, why do I have you on camera turning off the motorway on the A4 towards Bundary? I know the answer to my own question because you didn't drive straight home at all.

'Let me put it to you that you drove to Helen's house and if you don't start to tell us the truth, you are going to be spending at least the next twenty fours here and possibly longer still.'

Paul's attitude visibly changed as he completely caved in.

'Alright, alright, I did drive to Helen's house but I had absolutely nothing to do with the murder. My reason for going was to pay over some money.

'That asshole boyfriend of hers Oliver Traves had caught us in a hotel and filmed us in bed together. He said that unless I paid a ransom of five thousand pounds, he would make sure that my wife and three daughters would see the video.

'I cannot believe how I have got myself into this mess. My wife has had some cancer problems and following that she has completely gone off sex. I am still a relatively young man and couldn't stand the thought of never having sex again.

'For some strange reason, going out with someone from an escort agency seemed a little less seedy than going with a prostitute. Helen also happened to be a really sweet girl who understood my situation without judging me.

'It turned out she had her own marital problems, desperately wanted children but her husband was apparently infertile so it was impossible.

'He worked away from home a lot and inevitably they grew apart. I genuinely started to fall in love with this girl and I think she had feelings for me but for some reason this horrible low life drug pusher Oliver Traves had her under his spell.

'I know she set up the escort service with Mary Robins to earn a bit of money on the side but they were only really in it to have a bit of fun. I think they were incredibly naïve and didn't realise that going to bed with the client was going to be part of the deal.

'I am convinced that Traves encouraged them to keep the business going and saw himself as some self-styled pimp.

'Certainly, he set me up because Helen had told him which hotel we were going to and he waited until we were in bed then just kicked in the bedroom door.

'There was a fight and to be honest, I was no physical match for him. He said that unless I paid the money, the video would go viral.

'I just couldn't risk my whole world coming down on top of me, so I agreed to pay and that is why I was at Helen's house.'

Ray decided to go for the jugular.

'Yes, and what I think happened next is that when you took the money to Helen's house you got into an altercation with Oliver Traves, took a knife to him and Helen, trying to stop you got in the way. Is that what happened, Paul, because, if it did, we are going to find out so you may as well tell us the truth now.'

Paul was sweating profusely and made everyone jump as he slammed his hands down on the desk.

'No, no, no, that is not what happened at all. Much as I would have liked to stick a knife in that dickhead of a man, I didn't. I paid the money; he deleted the video on his phone and I left.

'That is exactly what happened and unless you are going to charge me with something, I need to be on my way.'

His confident arrogance reappeared as he got up to leave.

Ray nodded to let him go and noticed, as Paul Mason signed the visitor's book that he was left-handed.

Ray and Mike had called a meeting with Sally Marshall, Bob Sheldon, Bob Mitchell and the rest of the team for a working lunch after the interview with Paul Mason.

Ray opened up with an apology.

'Look, guys, sorry for dragging you in on a Sunday, but as we all know there is no such thing as the weekend in police work when a murder has been committed.

'You are all acutely aware that time is of the essence and every day that passes, the trail gets colder. It is exactly a week ago yesterday that this murder took place and I think it is time for us to evaluate exactly where we are with this case.

'Who had the motive, who had the opportunity and who are our suspects?

'Motive first, over to you Bob.'

'As you may remember from when we met last week that there are seven main reasons for homicide, the main ones being, not in any particular order, revenge, jealousy, hate, thrill and gain.

'I think we all agree that the main suspect is Oliver Traves but he doesn't seem to fit the profile except maybe gain. He does, however, have perfect opportunity.

'The husband Danny Maguire does come under the spotlight somewhat more in that, revenge, jealousy and hate could all apply to him.

'Jealousy, because he couldn't father a child owing to his low sperm count.

'Hatred, because his wife was pregnant with another man's baby, although he denies knowing this.

'Revenge, in that he killed her and the baby at the same time.

'However, if he is to be believed, there is a problem with opportunity because he maintains he never left the cricket ground.

'Finally, the man you interviewed this morning, Paul Mason, could also fit the profile of revenge, jealousy and hate.'

Ray thanked Bob for his appraisal and invited Bob Mitchell to give his overall thoughts on the forensic evidence.

'From the limited forensic evidence we have, I think we can rule out a random break-in. The five thousand pounds found in the drier could have been a motive, but we are now fairly certain that this was ransom money paid by Paul Mason.

'There are no defence wounds, whatsoever, on Helen's body, which indicates that she knew her killer and was not expecting to be attacked.

'The angle entry of the knife suggests someone definitely right-handed and fairly tall. This doesn't help a lot as more than three quarters of the population are right-handed.

'What does help a lot is that it appears the knife was thrust into the body with some force, so anger appears to have been present. The knife was also thrust into Helen's womb, which could have been an attempt to kill the foetus as well as her.'

Ray thanked Bob for his thoughts and suggested that as Sally was the senior crime investigator, her thoughts would be very useful to know.

'From what I have learned from the people down at the "Wet Whistle" pub, this Oliver Traves is a very nasty piece of work. He has a very short fuse, a violent temper, he is a known drug dealer, this is a very big and he has taken flight and disappeared to who knows where.

'The only thing that doesn't fit the bill, is if he murdered Helen in cold blood why didn't he take the money?

'It's possible that he wasn't there at all when Paul Mason arrived with the money; Helen hid it in the spin drier, they subsequently had a massive argument; he murdered her in anger and fled the scene.

'Oliver Traves may then have arrived late to the planned meeting with Paul Mason, saw the dead body on the kitchen floor, panicked and fled the scene.

'Unfortunately, we will never know whose fingerprints were on the murder weapon because Danny Maguire removed the knife from Helen's body.

'I hear what you say about the husband, but would he really plan to murder his own wife during the middle of a cricket match? You have to admit it does sound a little far-fetched.'

Mike Salter had said very little throughout the whole meeting and Ray took the opportunity to ask him his opinions.

'Well, there is no doubt in my mind that there are only three people in the frame for this murder, the drug dealer Oliver Traves, the husband Danny Maguire and the man we interviewed this morning, Paul Mason.

'I personally think Oliver Traves is our man for the simple reason that if he were innocent why would he flee the scene? We know he was there on the Saturday from the fingerprints on the coffee cup and he had motive. We are still looking for him but he may well have fled the country never to be seen again.

'The husband Danny Maguire is a strong candidate and certainly has motive but did he really have time to leave the ground, commit the murder, then return?

167

'Paul Mason also has motive and opportunity. He lied to us about his whereabouts but if he had killed Helen, either accidentally or not, why would he have left the money?'

With all his years of experience, Ray Stephens had learnt the art of listening to opinions, sorting the wheat from the chaff and had a knack of summing up matters with amazing clarity.

'I agree with everything that has been said and for one reason or another we may never solve this murder. As you all know there are roughly five hundred homicides in the U.K every year of which only forty percent reach conviction. Ten per cent of murders never reach prosecution and our case may well end up in that category.

'But as you all know, I never give up without a fight and I am determined that we look under every stone, uncover every scrap of evidence and follow every lead that we possibly can, before we call it a day.

'For that reason, I want to us to try and rule out the husband by proving that he never left the ground and therefore could not have committed the crime or prove that he did leave the ground and therefore become the prime suspect.

'We have literally hundreds of photographs taken on the day that may shed some light on his movements and also some video footage to go through.

'With regard to Paul Mason, let's look further into his background and see if he has been as squeaky clean in the past as he is making out.

It was time to call it a day and the officers slowly drifted away, leaving Ray and Mike discussing the case.

Ray appeared frustrated that little progress had been made and was keen to share his frustration with Mike.

'You know, Mike, I am still convinced that there is more to this case than meets the eye. The fact that the girls had set up this "Charm on Your Arm" escort agency sheds a brand-new light on potential suspects that at this stage we don't know anything about.

'I think we need to get Helen's partner Mary Robins back in again and find out whether there were other shady characters involved other than this guy Paul Mason. Drugs, sex and illicit affairs are all components of a dangerous lifestyle.

'It is still only just over a week since the murder took place and no doubt more information will come to light over the coming days.

'Let's leave it for now and dig a bit deeper into those photos and video film next week. Oh, and by the way, I wonder how our friends from the national crime squad are getting on with "Operation Mainline". I think it is today that the drugs are supposed to be arriving in Montenegro.

'Joe Willets and Andy Carter are over there working with the Montenegrin drug squad and I just hope that Jack Reed hasn't taken on more than he can chew in agreeing to help.'

Little did they know that their prime suspect, Oliver Traves had been shot, cut up on a band saw and fed to some hungry pigs on a small country farm somewhere between Dubrovnik and Montenegro.

Chapter Twelve

The dawn chorus outside Jack's bedroom was building to a crescendo as the birds competed for potential mates on a beautiful sunny spring morning.

He came round slowly and was pleased that his head wasn't thumping like a tin drum after consuming so much wine the night before. Opening the shutters, he appreciated that the setting of the vineyard was stunning.

The rows of vines fitted in perfectly with the lakes and the fields that surrounded the villa but the real beauty lay in the stillness of the place.

There were no sounds of machinery or cars rushing by and although it had only just started getting light, Jack decided to go for a walk.

He couldn't believe that so much had happened in just over a week and that his life had been completely turned on its head by a bizarre set of events.

He was in a very philosophical mood and wondered whether he would ever meet anyone again as special as Helen. Although he had only known her for a short time, there was chemistry between them that he had never felt with anyone else.

He was, of course, unaware that Helen hadn't exactly led a sheltered life and in addition to the affair with Oliver Traves she had set up an escort agency with her friend Mary Robins.

He had no regrets whatsoever that he had been responsible for setting up the death of Oliver Traves. As far as Jack was concerned, he was a low life piece of trash and was almost certainly responsible for Helen's murder.

He did, however, feel guilty about coming on to her and the pain that her husband Danny must be going through. Dealing drugs for two years and thinking of running off with a mate's wife wasn't exactly a code of conduct he had been brought up to follow.

He had never really considered that selling cocaine to people who were grateful for it was a bad thing. He thought it was crazy that a recreational drug that made people feel good was outlawed by society and that it was only a matter of time before its use was legalised.

He understood that heroin, crystal meth, LSD and other class A drugs were highly dangerous but he had never known anyone who had died from taking small amounts of cocaine.

He did, however, recognise the addictive nature of drugs and alcohol and had come close to being dependent on both. His stomach tightened as he realised the enormity of what he had become involved in.

Today was indeed judgment day, one hundred kilos of pure cocaine with a street value in the region of ten million pounds was at this very moment hidden aboard a twenty-metre yacht slowly working its way up the Albanian coastline.

For its size, the value of the consignment was staggering, as it took comparatively very little space to hide the equivalent of one hundred bags of sugar. This was one of the main reasons why only five per cent of drug production was ever found and confiscated by the authorities.

It was amazing that cocaine could be bought for two dollars a gram in Colombia and yet sold for up to one hundred dollars a gram in New York. It was indeed one of the few markets with an enormous profit margin. He completely understood why the Vukovic brothers had become more interested in the drug trade rather than producing wine.

He also had more than a twinge of guilt that his undercover work would help bring down the Vukovic empire. On the word of Nikolay, they had invited him into their home and trusted his involvement in their business. They had all seemed very genuine and likeable people.

He was also more than aware that if he had done the job of ferrying the drugs back to England for just two years, he would have earned almost a quarter of a million pounds without paying a penny in tax. He could have paid off the mortgage on his house by the age of twenty-five and then got out of the drug trade completely.

Then a reality check, because on the other hand, he could have ended up in prison for a very long time, the drug trade truly was the epitome of risk and reward.

As he made his way slowly between the vines, one of the house dogs joined him and obviously enjoyed a morning stroll with anyone it could latch onto.

Jack started to feel anxious that today could mark the end of a highly lucrative business. He knew that whilst closing down one route of importation, another would spring up very quickly somewhere else.

He thought it was similar to trying to stop a river that was in flood. As soon as one area was protected, another would be breached. It reminded him of a story he had once read about a little Dutch boy who put his finger in a dyke in an effort to save his village.

He began to worry that the police may not be able to track the drugs once they were transferred from the yacht. He had assumed that they would be transported directly to the vineyard and hidden there, but that may not be the case.

It was possible that the consignment could be hidden in a farm or a warehouse somewhere until the brothers felt safe about shipping it out to their dealers throughout Europe.

He wondered how the police would surround the vineyard and be certain of arresting all the members of the gang. He wasn't even sure whether the Vukovic brothers would remain at the villa. They had stayed there on Saturday night after the meal but their main homes were in a village to the north of Podgorica.

Whilst he hadn't seen any evidence of guns, he thought it was highly likely there would be some firearm protection in a villa that was in such a remote location.

As he walked towards the two warehouse buildings at the rear of the villa Nikolay appeared from nowhere and beckoned him over.

'Good morning, Jack, I hope you slept well and are not suffering the ill effects of drinking too much wine last night. Come let me show you the big vats in which the wine is stored.'

They entered the building, which contained three massive tanks, each at least five metres high and capable of holding six thousand gallons of wine.

Nikolay was keen to give Jack a tour of the facility and show off his knowledge of wine making.

'So, this is the engine room, in a few months from now these tanks will be fermenting our delicious wine. For now, they just contain water. I think you would agree that it is a little different to how they used to tread grapes years ago.

'This industry has progressed in lock step with farming and now uses mechanical harvesters that straddle the grapevine trellises and shake the grapes free from the stems. As you can imagine this saves an enormous amount of time and effort.'

Jack wasn't really in the mood to have a full-blown lesson on wine making and suggested it was time for breakfast.

As they entered the dining room, Dragan and Josif were already seated and tucking into a light meal of assorted cheeses and meats and mugs of strong-smelling coffee.

Josif was first to speak.

'Good morning, Jack, I notice you go for long walk around vineyard. Very peaceful and good time to enjoy the scenery and fresh air.

'Hope you enjoy meal last night and also the wine. It has been drunk for over nine thousand years now by us humans and let's hope it will be drunk for next nine thousand years. This morning we open bottle of champagne to celebrate arrival of new baby so to speak.

'This is Dom Perignon, the finest of all champagnes and first produced in the seventeenth century by a monk of the same name.

'He invent secondary fermentation that cause the bubbles. You like?'

Josif poured everyone a glass of champagne and toasted the safe arrival of the goods that were currently en route along the Albanian Riviera.

There was a short-wave radio crackling away on the breakfast table and Jack assumed that the brothers were in contact with the captain of the yacht.

Josif seemed to read Jack's mind and decided to put him in the picture.

'We speak to the captain Zivko a few minutes ago and he say that all is well and the yacht is scheduled to arrive here mid-afternoon. I think you will be on way back to England with four kilos on Monday, Nikolay take two kilos to Macca in Dubrovnik and Spiridon four kilos to our man in Belgrade.

'Then everybody happy and everything rosy in garden.'

Taking another sip of champagne, he chuckled to himself and seemed to talk about the distribution of a highly illegal substance as though it was just another ordinary grocery item such as sugar or salt.

Indeed, Zivko Bekic and his crew of two were thoroughly enjoying the trip from Orikum up to the Bay of Kotor.

Zivko had a skin that had been weathered by the sun and the salt from the sea. He had joined the navy in the year two thousand and six just as conscription ended and the Montenegrin navy was established.

He was very proud of the fact that over a ten-year period he had worked his way up to the rank of captain and he liked nothing better than the challenge of sailing a yacht in choppy waters and a strong wind.

The Lepo Grozde was, however, a motor yacht not a traditional sailing boat and could reach speeds of up to twenty-five knots. It was fitted with all the new modern equipment such as GPS or global positioning system, a radar scanner and even a fish finder chartplotter.

Zivko had even worked out that at his current speed and distance remaining to Kotor Bay that he would arrive at exactly 3.56 p.m.

Although the Vukovic brothers owned the Lepo Grozde, Zivko treated it as his own and maintained the boat in immaculate condition. He travelled out to Colombia with Spiridon Ilic and once the cocaine had been purchased, he stayed with the cargo for the whole journey back to Montenegro.

It was important that someone kept a watchful eye on such a valuable consignment from beginning to end and ensured that all documentation was in order for the various port authorities.

As there were only two consignments a year, each taking about ten weeks to complete, Zivko was very happy with his workload. He was paid one hundred thousand American dollars per trip to oversee the operation from beginning to end and had earned in one year as much as he had earned for all his years in the navy.

The goods were cleverly hidden under the floorboards in one of the yacht's bedrooms. A bed that looked fixed to the floor, actually folded up to the wall to expose an area under which the drugs were carefully placed.

No one seemed particularly anxious that a ten-million-dollar consignment was on its way because no one was aware that behind the scenes plans were being made in Podgorica that would ensure that, if successful, the Vukovic brothers would not be enjoying champagne again for many years to come.

It had been an early start for Joe Willets and Andy Carter as they were driven the short distance from their hotel to the four-storey police headquarters in the centre of Podgorica.

The drug enforcement squad was housed on the third floor and was a hive of activity when Joe and Andy arrived.

Janko beckoned the two men over to the area where two officers were in charge of ensuring that the overhead drone was working properly.

The officers, in their early twenties, were graduates of the University of Montenegro and had both achieved "Firsts" in engineering technology, a course that majored in advanced electronic communications and applied computer sciences.

At a cost of seventeen million dollars the government had invested in the latest technology and bought a top of the range military drone, which boasted a four-metre wingspan and could stay in the air for up to fourteen hours.

The young men had both spent three months in the United States learning how to operate the drone before it had become serviceable in Montenegro.

They spoke perfect English and were obviously extremely proud of being in charge of such a modern addition to policing.

Joe and Andy learnt that drones were first used in the war in Afghanistan in two thousand and thirteen and measured just one inch by four inches. They were called black hornets because that is exactly what they looked like and were used by the military to look round corners and over walls.

Drone technology had come on in leaps and bounds since then and from the early days when drones were principally used for surveillance, it was now possible to buy military style drone planes that could operate at thirty-five thousand feet and destroy anything on the ground within accuracy of a metre.

The drone currently flying over the Lepo Grozde yacht at a height of three thousand feet was affectionately known as "Eagle Eye".

The senior of the two drone operators was known as the ground station remote controller and he was keen to share his knowledge with Joe and Andy.

'Gentlemen, "Eagle Eye" is what we call a MALE drone, the acronym being short for medium altitude long endurance.

'So, this young bird can fly up to a height of ten thousand feet at speeds of up to two hundred miles per hour and stay in the air for fourteen hours. Some of the new military drones can reach speeds in excess of a thousand miles per hour and stay in the air for thirty-six hours.

'But the real sophistication in this surveillance drone is in the advancement of camera technology.

'In addition to the infrared cameras allowing night vision, the telephoto lens allows real time video capture. The addition of a stabilisation gimbal allows for more accurate shots and also allows the camera to tilt at different angles whilst in flight.

'We receive super resolution pictures in vivid details to the point of facial recognition.'

Joe and Andy glanced at each other; probably both realising why these whizz kids had both obtained "Firsts" at university. Information technology, electronics, communications and computers had all moved on at an ever-increasing pace and way beyond their understanding.

The decision by the government to buy the drone had already paid off handsomely with Montenegro and Albania working together on joint projects.

The drone was ideal for surveillance in the mountainous regions of both countries and was instrumental in finding fields of cannabis plants, which was the principal drug grown in Albania. The problem was that as soon as one field had been identified and cleared by the authorities, another would spring up somewhere else.

Janko called his officers together and obviously, whilst addressing them in Montenegrin, was courteous enough to then translate into his best English for the benefit of Joe and Andy.

'Gentlemen, ladies, we welcome our friends today from England, Mr Joe Willets and Mr Andy Carter who both work for the UK National Crime Agency in conjunction with Interpol on "Operation Mainline".

'This operation is to stop the importation of drugs from the Balkans into mainland Britain.

'They have an undercover man who has been accepted into gang and at this moment is awaiting delivery of drugs at vineyard in Virpazar near Lake Skadar. His job is to travel to England by train with four kilos of pure cocaine in back pack.

'The drugs have come from Colombia by boat, hidden in furniture and ending up in Durres port in Albania. From there they transfer to motor yacht in marina in Orikum in South of country.

'Today that yacht called Lepo Grozde is moving up coast to the Bay of Kotor where drugs will then be transferred to the vineyard. We estimate size of shipment to be in region of one hundred kilos with street value of ten million pounds. Our job

179

is to follow the drugs all the way to final resting place, seize them and arrest people involved. Sound very simple but as we know can be big difficult.'

Janko paused for breath and looked round the room to gauge a reaction from his officers.

There were at least half a dozen female officers present, as they tended to be better at undercover work than men but were still fully trained up in all aspects of drug enforcement.

In total Janko had a task force of some thirty people at his disposal and appeared keen to get on with his presentation.

'So now I outline plan to make sure this mission not fail. First, I manage to get use of our two Gazelle helicopters based at Golubovci airport in Podgorica.

'I have to go down on my knees to beg Ministry of Internal Affairs to allow us to have them.

'With vineyard nearly a square mile in size there is no way we can risk going in by car. There are two massive gates at entrance and if they do not let us in, we could lose the advantage of surprise. By the time we blow gates with explosive they could hide the drugs anywhere on the estate or worse still destroy them before we get to them.

'Surprise will be everything and nothing better than two helicopters landing at entrance to villa at same time. We have studied landing site and no problem with trees for helicopters.

'The helicopters are five-seater so we have four armed men in each one and they storm the villa and gain control of situation. As far as we know there will not be more than about six people at the villa so eight armed officers should be able to control situation. We do not expect armed conflict but must be prepared if it happens.

'The airport is only twenty kilometres from vineyard and ten minutes flying time so we can be there before they know what is happening.

'As soon as officers in villa, they will open gates to allow the four police cars outside to enter and surround all the buildings. We will not know exactly where the drugs will be stored but for sure there will be a hiding place as they will have a plan for surprise visit by police.'

There was a genuine feeling of excitement in the room as everyone realised the importance of getting everything right as the mission entered the final phases and Janko was keen to get on with finalising his presentation.

'So, we estimate that the Lepo Grozde at current speed will enter Montenegrin waters at around noon. At this point as well as being followed by "Eagle Eye", a car will follow boat along the coast road from Bar on the E80 to make sure it does not pull into any cove and unload drugs.

'The rear of Lepo Grozde has been adapted to have motorboat on board and we think that the drugs will be moved from main yacht to motorboat and then easy to get motorboat into small cove and drugs unload there.

'This probably be done in Kotor Bay as many holiday motorboats moving around so no one take notice. "Eagle Eye" will be able to see from sky if packages moved into motorboat and follow from there.

'We will also have motorboat in Kotor Bay so that we can follow them at a distance and keep another pair of eyes on them.

'The drugs will probably be transferred to SUV type of vehicle and then hopefully taken direct to vineyard in Virpazar.

'After motorboat return and fixed back to Lepo Grozde it will probably berth in usual place in Porto Montenegro.

'We will have two plain-clothes officers sitting in café that overlook harbour to see what captain and crew do after they have secured the Lepo Grozde to its berth.

'The undercover informer working for British police has with him a very clever phone that can listen in on conversations.

'Unfortunately, no mast in remote Virpazar can pick up signal so we learn nothing from him.

'However, he does have very clever money clip which has built-in radio transmitter.

'The plan is that when drugs arrive, the informer activates money clip transmitter and that is our cue for operation to start.

'Hopefully we shall also know from "Eagle Eye" that drugs are being unloaded at the villa.'

A few questions were asked by the officers but to all intents and purposes all bases had been covered. Short wave radio sets were handed out to all operatives and tested to ensure that they were working properly.

Joe and Andy were extremely impressed with the work that had gone on behind the scenes at such short notice and also the amount of resource that had been invested in the operation.

They had been made to feel incredibly welcome, and as ever in a foreign country, impressed with how many people spoke English. They did not speak a word of Montenegrin and probably never would.

The waiting game was always the hardest part of any operation and as it was still only mid-morning there were a few hours to kill before the real action began.

Janko, Joe and Andy decided to go to a local café and enjoy a brunch before returning for an afternoon that would hopefully see a successful climax to taking down a multimillion-pound drug operation that would certainly make international news headlines.

Heading for the door, they couldn't help glancing across at the computer monitor showing incredible pictures of the Lepo Grozde making its way north through the choppy waters of the Albanian coastline with the crew on board totally oblivious to the "Eagle Eye" three thousand feet above them.

With all the pieces of the jigsaw now in place what could possibly go wrong?

Chapter Thirteen

At exactly 4.00 p.m. the Lepo Grozde entered the sheltered waters of Kotor Bay. The bay, considered to be one of the most beautiful in the world was forged between two mountain regions, one to the west and one to the east.

With a length of approximately twenty-seven kilometres, a shoreline of over one hundred kilometres and a depth of forty metres, the bay was a Mecca for travel and in particular cruise ships.

In recent times it had become the ideal place to entice clients away from the overcrowded harbours of the Riviera and the Italian Adriatic.

Part Norwegian grandeur, part spa retreat and part Monaco style tourist trap the whole area had become a hotspot for investment and a burgeoning holiday industry.

The crystal-clear waters of the fjord boasted over a thousand species of fish, which thrived among the many islands, dotted about in the bay.

With sunset at 6.00 p.m. the normally frenetic activity of boats was starting to slow down with trips to the famous islands of "Our Lady of The Rock" and "St George" returning home.

It was just as everyone in the control room in Podgorica was gathered around the monitors watching the Lepo Grozde edging its way along the coastline towards Porto Montenegro that things started to go wrong.

For no apparent reason the images from the drone started to become blurred and indistinguishable. The technicians were desperately trying to resolve the problems but nothing seemed to help. Battery level was checked and appeared fine, movement and speed were both controllable but whatever slight changes to the cameras were made, nothing improved the pictures they were receiving.

Nobody could believe what was happening, "Eagle Eye" had worked perfectly for ten hours and had followed the Lepo Grozde all two hundred or so miles from Orikum in Albania to the Bay of Kotor, without a single hitch.

Just at the point where it was most needed and the drugs were to be transferred ashore "Eagle Eye" appeared literally to be on the blink.

Janko grabbed one of the short-wave radio sets and contacted his two officers stationed on the speedboat looking out for the arrival of the Lepo Grozde.

Fortunately, they had high-powered binoculars on board and already spotted the yacht edging its way up the coastline. He instructed them to move close enough to see what was going on but not too close to arouse suspicion.

With the whizz kids still trying to solve the problems with the drone; Janko was incredibly grateful that he still had eyes on the target and could monitor the situation.

After what seemed an eternity but was probably less than twenty minutes, the officers reported that the crew had appeared to be off-loading goods into the speedboat attached to the rear the Lepo Grozde.

Shortly after, the speedboat was released and accelerated off towards land. Janko ordered his men to follow and report back with the heading they were on and feverishly searched around for a detailed map of the area.

With the heading relayed back he suddenly threw his arms up in the air and shouted out to no one in particular.

'I know exactly where they are going, they are heading towards the World War Two submarine pen.'

Turning to Joe and Andy, he explained that in the Second World War Germany had built submarine pens that were carved inside the natural hills of the coastline and used them as a bunker to protect their submarines from air attack.

Encased within concrete, they extended a few hundred metres into the hillside and were incredibly difficult to bomb with any success.

Janko could now see that the plan was to unload the goods at the end of the tunnel, whereby a series of steps led to an exit on top of the hill. From there a dirt track led through the scrub and eventually onto the main road.

No one could see from the water that on the dirt track at the top of the cliff was an old Land Rover capable of navigating off-road terrain.

The speedboat disappeared into the old submarine pen and within minutes had reappeared and was on the way back to the Lepo Grozde.

Janko was desperate to see what was going on but guessed that a vehicle must be involved in taking the drugs from the submarine pen but the problem was that he had no idea what make or type of vehicle that may be.

He was beginning to panic because there was now no aerial feed from the drone, whatsoever, and the decision had been taken to return it to Podgorica airport rather than risk potentially losing it altogether.

There were so many dirt tracks leading down from the coast that it was impossible to guess where the vehicle would eventually enter the main road. It was also totally impractical for him to ask his men to look out for the make of a vehicle he didn't know, moving in a direction north, east, south or west.

There was a dreadful atmosphere of failure in the control room as Janko decided to stand down the helicopter crews. There was absolutely no point in trying to guess when the drugs would arrive back at the vineyard if indeed that was the final hiding place.

He decided to keep a watchful eye on the lanes around the vineyard in the hope that that they may just be brought in through the main gates. As far as the Vukovic brothers knew, they were not under surveillance and therefore there was no reason to be ultra-cautious.

The team did, however, have one more ace up their sleeve as it had been agreed that if the drugs did arrive back at the vineyard, Jack would activate the radio transmitter that was built into his money clip. The helicopters could then be there, literally within minutes and everyone would be caught red-handed.

Once again, however, the best laid plans of mice and men were about to go wrong in a very unlucky turn of events.

The minutes had passed very slowly in the villa at Virpazar as everyone waited for news that the Lepo Grozde had indeed made it back to the Bay of Kotor and that the drugs had been successfully transferred and were on the way to the vineyard.

Dragan Vukovic had been in contact with the captain of the Lepo Grozde who was shortly to moor up the yacht in its usual berth in Porto Montenegro.

As ever, he was to be paid one hundred thousand American dollars, which included payment for his crew as well as the fact that Zivko had travelled all the way from Colombia keeping a watchful eye on the valuable cargo.

Macca had duly delivered the ten thousand dollars that Jack had hidden under the mattress of Oliver Traves and Nikolay now had the full one hundred thousand dollars that he had exchanged in Dubrovnik.

It had been agreed that the handover of the money would take place at 6.00 p.m. in the café Maprezzo in Porto Montenegro.

Dragan suggested that Nikolay take Jack along with him so that he could meet the captain and it would also kill a little bit of time whilst they waited for the drugs to arrive at the vineyard.

Jack's heart sank as he realised the whole plan depended upon him activating the radio transmitter at the very moment the drugs arrived. The police would be there within minutes and effectively the brothers would be caught red-handed.

Away from the vineyard, he would not have a clue what was going on and would not be able to help in anyway but he also had no good reason to stay behind. He grabbed his phone on the way out in the hope that he would be able to contact Andy Carter at some point whilst in Porto Montenegro.

Back at police headquarters in Podgorica, Janko's anxiety levels had reached new heights. He had lost his eyes in the sky and in addition he had no idea where the drugs were and when they would be delivered.

He also realised that he had one chance to get it right. Tomorrow the drugs could be hidden anywhere between Serbia and Croatia.

What he did know with some certainty was that the drugs had been on board the Lepo Grozde, he also knew with some certainty that they had been transferred by speedboat to the mainland.

More importantly there was no reason for anyone at the vineyard to think that the police had been following and watching the whole operation unfold.

He came to the conclusion that although no vehicle had been spotted going into the estate, an off-road jeep or truck could have used any of the tracks surrounding the grounds.

He estimated it would take approximately an hour to drive from the drop-off point at the submarine bunker back to the vineyard in Virpazar and decided that he would make his move at exactly 6.00 p.m. just as it was starting to get dark.

This would allow adequate time for the vehicle to get back to the vineyard but hopefully not enough time for the drugs to be hidden away. With the vineyard being almost a square mile in size, it did cross his mind that finding the drugs could be like trying to find the proverbial needle in a haystack.

It was time to gamble and he just had to hope and pray that today lady luck would be on his side. He called everyone together and announced that five police cars and twenty officers would descend on the vineyard at exactly 6.00 p.m. and if access was not granted, the gates would be blown open.

Nikolay and Jack arrived at the café Maprezzo just as diners were being seated for their evening meal. As ever Porto

Montenegro was buzzing with holidaymakers from all over the globe enjoying the food and ambience of a wonderful setting.

Zivko Bekic was sitting at a corner table and looked as nervous as a kitten until Nikolay reassuredly threw his arms around him. The couple had met the year before and Zivko seemed to lighten up somewhat as Jack was introduced to him and three black coffees were ordered.

Jack took the opportunity to go to the toilet, which fortunately was on the other side of the café. He now had a signal on his phone and immediately rang Andy Carter explaining he knew nothing of the whereabouts of the drugs as he had been sent with Nikolay to pay off the captain of the Lepo Grozde.

Andy explained that the drone had failed at exactly the wrong time but they were still going ahead with raiding the vineyard, as they were certain the drugs had been taken there.

Returning to the table, it was obvious that Zivko was not in the mood for any small talk and was more interested in making off with his bag containing the hundred thousand dollars.

At the very moment that Jack and Nikolay were paying for the drinks, five police cars were entering through the gates of the vineyard in Virpazar. There had been no drama when they had announced their presence and as they approached the villa in convoy, the Vukovic brothers were standing at the entrance to greet them.

Roughly translated Josif was the first to speak.

'Gentlemen, how nice to see so many police officers, I didn't know we were having a party tonight but if we are, you are most welcome to come inside.'

All twenty officers including Joe Willets and Andy Carter entered the villa. In addition, a unit with dogs specially trained in finding drugs, had been called in to help with the search.

First of all, every room, drawer and cupboard in the villa was searched. Carpets and rugs were lifted to ensure that nothing had been hidden under the floorboards. The voids above the ceilings were checked and chimneys were fully investigated.

The dogs didn't appear to be remotely interested in anything they sniffed and after an hour of intense searching by all twenty officers nothing but a dead bird up one of the chimneys had been found.

All the time, the Vukovic brothers, the accountant Spiridon Ilic and the vineyard manager Vlado Petrovic looked on with a complete lack of concern or interest.

The next building to be searched was the dilapidated garage that housed an old tractor and a few ancient farm implements but yet again there was nowhere that remotely resembled a potential hiding place.

As darkness started to close in, the search moved to the warehouse complex at the rear of the villa and Janko sensed that the brothers seemed to tense up a little. Parked alongside the warehouse was an old jeep, which could well have been used to ferry the drugs from the scrubland near the old submarine pen.

Inside the massive warehouse there were three large copper cylinders that would normally hold the wine but during the off-season they were mostly full of water to keep them clean.

Each cylinder was five metres high and had been formed by welding individual sheets of one metre copper together with pop rivets.

At first sight it wasn't possible to see how drugs could be stored in the cylinders, which were each more than half full of water.

Everyone was convinced that once the water was released, the drugs would be found wrapped in waterproof packaging at the base of the units, unfortunately torchlight revealed nothing but shiny copper bottoms and a small residue of slurry.

After a thorough search of the whole warehouse complex had been completed, everyone was about to give up, but just as they were leaving, Joe Willets suggested to Janko that it was just possible that because welding individual sheets of copper together had formed the cylinders, that one of them could have a false bottom.

The only way this could be ascertained was to dangle a weight on the end of a five-metre line from the top of the cylinder and see if it reached the bottom.

A ball of string was eventually found in the workshop, measured out to five metres and attached to a rusty old spanner. The first two cylinders were exactly five metres in depth but the third came up a metre short.

All the pop rivet caps were examined and low and behold at the base of the third cylinder, four of the rivet heads were found to be removable and underneath were four everyday slotted head screws.

Removing the screws, revealed a one metre square panel, which just happened to contain, neatly stacked on top of one another, about one hundred neatly wrapped packages, each the approximate size of a kilo bag of sugar.

Janko couldn't resist cracking a joke.

'Gentlemen, it would appear that we have found the children's Christmas presents.'

Whilst there was massive relief among the team of police officers, there were no dramatic scenes. One of the packages was tested and sure enough was proved to contain cocaine at its highest purity.

Some of the staff were in tears as the Vukovic brothers, the accountant Spiridon Ilic and the vineyard manager Vlado Petrovic were all handcuffed and lead out of the villa to the waiting police cars.

As they were read their rights, they appeared to take their fate philosophically and seemed more concerned about who was going to secure the villa than contacting their lawyer.

Janko insisted that the packages were all counted in front of him, as he wasn't taking any chances with one or two going missing en route back to Podgorica.

With each package having a street value of approximately one hundred thousand dollars, this was temptation at its worst.

Completely oblivious to what had happened in the last couple of hours, Jack and Nikolay had arrived back to the vineyard to find the gates suspiciously wide open.

Edging their way up the drive, with the headlights on the car turned off, they could see that all the villa lights were ablaze and police officers were everywhere.

They arrived just in time to see the Vukovic brothers being bundled into the back of the police cars and had just about enough time to turn the car round and disappear into the night, at the rate of knots.

Nikolay was close to tears as he sped off away from the vineyard.

'Oh my God, Jack, it looks as though the game is well and truly up. What on earth are we going to do now?'

It was a statement more than a question because the shock of what Nikolay had witnessed seemed to stun him into a trance as he stared into the fading light and negotiated the country lanes at high speed.

Jack suggested that they return to Porto Montenegro and disappear amongst the many tourists, as there was no reason why the police would be looking for them. Nikolay appeared to slowly come out of his trance and agreed that the police might not even know of their existence.

They both had their credit cards, passports and phones with them so apart from some clothes back at the vineyard, there were no signs of them ever being there.

Jack had to find a way of convincing Nikolay that they would be better off splitting up and going their separate ways. As Nikolay had the hire car, it made sense for him to return to Dubrovnik and hide out with Macca until the dust had settled, whilst he would return to England as planned by train.

Nikolay seemed to warm to the idea and even apologised to Jack for having a wasted trip to Montenegro and the planned assignment never even getting off the ground. Needless to say, Jack was relieved that no suspicion seemed to fall on him for the detection of the plan to bring the drugs into the country.

Once back in Porto Montenegro, they chose a restaurant near the harbour and settled down for a final meal together.

Looking out over the array of super yachts in front of them Nikolay couldn't help but see the irony in what had happened.

'You know, Jack, it was only the greed of wanting to own one of those yachts that caused their downfall. The brothers owned a successful and legitimate wine business, a beautiful vineyard and a lovely lifestyle, but even that wasn't enough in the end.

'Why do people push the boundaries when they have spent half their life digging their way out of the backstreets of poverty? Maybe it's just human nature to always want more.

'Now they will spend many years in prison, have their property and goods confiscated and regret ever thinking they could outwit the authorities.

'Maybe this is a lesson to us that the strong arm of the law does eventually catch up and it's time to move onto something legitimate.'

Jack was beginning to feel incredibly guilty that it was only because of his involvement that everything had turned out the way it had. If Nikolay knew the truth about his collusion in the brother's downfall, he would almost certainly end up with a bullet in the back of his head.

Nikolay decided that, as it was only a two-hour drive back to Dubrovnik, he would contact Macca and spend some time with him, before making his next move. Although there was no reason why the Montenegrin police would be looking for him, he felt as though he wanted to put some distance between himself and the Vukovic brothers.

Jack told Nikolay that as he had made his mind up to return to the UK by train, he was going to buy a few casual clothes and a rucksack in Porto Montenegro before the shops closed.

He would then catch a late bus to Podgorica; stay the night there, before setting off for Belgrade the following day on the first leg of his journey home.

What he failed to add was that he was going to meet up with the police officers from the UK who had been instrumental in his involvement from the word go.

There were hugs and handshakes when they finally left the restaurant and promises to keep in touch, but they were both aware that it was highly unlikely their paths would ever cross again.

As soon as Nikolay was out of sight Jack phoned Andy Carter to get an update on what had transpired at the vineyard and whether the drugs had been found.

Andy said he would put him in the picture with everything that had happened when they met up and explained that he was in a restaurant with Joe Willets, Janko Kovac and about two-dozen Montenegrin drug squad officers all celebrating the success of the operation.

Although it was getting late, Andy explained that there was a carnival atmosphere developing and the party was likely to continue for quite a while. He suggested that Jack join them and in the meantime, he would book him a room for the night in their hotel.

Jack finally arrived at the restaurant just before midnight and the party was indeed in full swing. He couldn't understand a word of what was being spoken and kept a low profile as none of the officers were aware that he was indeed the undercover agent who had infiltrated the gang.

He was brought up to speed with how things had gone wrong in the latter stages of the operation when they had communication problems with the drone, resulting in them losing sight of the drug transfer just at the critical time.

Nevertheless, they had decided to take a risk that the consignment had been hidden somewhere in the vineyard. After a search of the villa uncovered nothing, they moved to the warehouse and discovered a false compartment in one of the huge wine vats with just enough space to conceal one hundred kilos of cocaine.

It appeared that the two tech guys were getting a dreadful ribbing over the failure of the drone in the latter stages of the operation and Janko couldn't help joining in the fun.

'We have military drone costing seventeen million dollars, the use of two Gazelle helicopters and in the end a ball of string and a rusty old spanner save the day.'

Everyone burst out laughing, as the two tech guys were drenched in beer by a couple of the young officers who were getting decidedly over-happy.

Andy and Joe were full of praise for Jack and the part he had played. He too had a dig at the state-of-the-art phone he had been given, which nobody had realised didn't work without a mobile signal and he also returned the radio transmitter money clip which had not been needed.

There were no questions with regard to the whereabouts of Nikolay as now the supply source had been closed down; he was effectively out of a job. Jack did, however, mention that the Bristol CID should be informed that Oliver Traves had been eliminated as a casualty of the drug trade.

Arrangements for the return to the UK were discussed and Jack was offered a seat on the same plane as Andy and Joe leaving Podgorica airport the following afternoon.

'Guys, I appreciate the offer but I have decided that this is a great opportunity for me to travel back by train and see some of the finest scenery Europe has to offer.

'Apparently, the Bar to Belgrade railway is one of the most scenic train journeys in the world and it leaves Podgorica at 10.00 a.m. in the morning arriving Belgrade at 8.00 p.m.

'It is three hundred miles long and boasts two hundred and fifty-four tunnels and four hundred and thirty-five bridges. It sounds a truly wonderful trip and this is a great opportunity for me to see a part of the world I may not be revisiting for quite a while.

'From Belgrade I will decide to either go back to the UK via Budapest, Vienna and Brussels or go the shorter route via Zagreb, Zurich and Paris.

'Either way, it sounds a fantastic journey and it will allow me to spend time in some different cities I have never seen.'

Andy and Joe seemed genuinely envious of such a trip but didn't think their bosses would extend their gratitude to a return train journey through eastern and central Europe.

Jack suddenly felt exhausted as the events of the last few days caught up with him and he decided it was time to call it a day.

The overnight hotel was only a short walk from the restaurant and having agreed to catch up with Joe and Andy when he was back in the UK, he quietly slipped away into the cool midnight air.

Crawling into bed he looked back on ten days of madness that had started with a cricket match in a small village on the outskirts of Bristol and ended with a ten-million-pound drugs haul in a country he had barely heard of.

In between, there had been the senseless murder of a beautiful young woman with whom he had fallen in love and the loss of an unborn child, which he may well have fathered. At least he had got his revenge with the elimination of Oliver Traves.

Only the night before he had been dining with two brothers who thought they were above the law but they had now drunk their last glass of champagne for many years to come. Tonight, they were getting used to a prison cell in Podgorica instead of a warm comfortable bed.

It had been a roller-coaster ride for sure and as he drifted off to sleep his thoughts returned to Helen and the life they could have had together.

Chapter Fourteen

The following day, just as Jack Reed was boarding the 10.00 a.m. train from Podgorica to Belgrade a meeting was about to start at the police headquarters in Portishead.

News of the successful drug raid in Montenegro and the death of Oliver Traves had filtered through to Ray Stephens and Mile Salter who had called the team together for a briefing.

Ray kicked off the meeting with his customary analysis of how he thought the case was going.

'Good morning, folks, and firstly it may interest you to know that I had a phone call this morning from Joe Willets of the national crime squad informing me of a successful conclusion to "Operation Mainline" in the Balkans.

'Apparently, Jack Reed was able to infiltrate the gang and pass on details of when and where the drugs were arriving and the names of the principal drug members. It has resulted in the seizure of one of the largest consignments of cocaine ever discovered in Montenegro.

'Needless to say, Jack has become somewhat of a hero and any charges that were being brought against him have been dropped.

'Unfortunately, our prime suspect to the murder of Helen Maguire became a casualty of the operation with Oliver Traves apparently being chopped up and fed to some hungry pigs at a farm just outside of Dubrovnik.

'Obviously, it would be a very tidy ending to our case if we could prove one way or another that Oliver Traves had committed the murder.

'Unfortunately, that is not the situation and we have to press on with the evidence we have left.

'As I have said before, we may never solve this case but before it is closed, I want us to be sure that we have examined every single clue, followed every single lead and examined every piece of evidence that we could.

'Let's examine what we have learnt in the last ten days and then see what remains to be investigated further.

'Firstly, we have good forensic evidence that the murder was committed sometime between 2.30 p.m. and 4.00 p.m. which rules out Jack Reed because we know he was on the cricket field for the whole of that time.

'We have also pretty much ruled out that this may have been a random break-in, because if it had been, I am sure the five thousand pounds in the spin drier would have been found and lifted. In addition, the fact there were no defence wounds, pretty much proves that Helen knew her attacker.

'That leaves us with three prime suspects, Oliver Traves, Paul Mason and the husband Danny Maguire. We have no forensic evidence; we have no CCTV but we do have a library full of photos taken on the day and also a video that may yield something of interest.

'I also think that we can rule out Paul Mason, as he is lefthanded which does not fit the profile of the knife attack.

He has no criminal record and I think he was just the victim of an unfortunate liaison.

'I genuinely think he went round to the house to pay the ransom money and that was the end of his involvement.

'I want the whole team to spend the day searching through what we have got. I don't know what we are looking for but let's do some real police work and see what we can find.'

One of the itches that Ray had to keep scratching was the fact that when the husband Danny was first interviewed about the murder, he kept saying that he had a cast iron alibi because he could recall all the details of what had happened over by over.

He even went through how the fall of each wicket had happened proving his presence at the ground at the time of the murder.

It just seemed a strange thing to say when he hadn't been accused of anything and immediately put an element of doubt in Ray's mind.

Whilst a team of six officers started to search through all the photos that had been collected, Ray decided to have a look through the scorebooks that were used on the matchday.

From the word go, it was obvious that the Fieldhouses scorer Allison Bunfield was the more proficient in that every detail was neatly entered and all the information, including a timeline, formed a perfect catalogue of the match as it progressed.

In comparing the two scorebooks Ray suddenly noticed that that there was one glaring difference between them. In the Fieldhouses scorebook alongside the name of Bob Short, it was noted that the wicket keeper stumped him but in the Bundary scorebook, it was noted that he was run out.

This meant that one of the entries was wrong because there was a subtle, but very real difference, between the two methods of dismissal.

Ray decided to scratch the itch a little bit more and phoned Allison Bunfield to get a definitive answer. She remembered the incident perfectly and explained that because the Bundary scorer, Sarah Miles, was relatively inexperienced; she probably didn't understand the difference between a run out and a stumping.

Allison explained that the batsman, Bob Short, overbalanced from the batting crease and the wicket keeper whipped off the bails from the stumps and this was known as a stumping.

This was a totally different thing to being run out which was simply when a batsman did not run the distance between the two wickets before the bails were removed.

Allison then mentioned something that got Ray's full attention.

'Danny arrived about forty-five minutes or so before tea and I'm surprised he didn't correct Sarah's mistake when he came into the scorebox because he must have spent ten minutes looking through the scorebook before leaving.

'I thought he had come just to make sure she was doing the job properly but he made no corrections to the book whilst he was there.'

Ray thanked Allison for her help and his thoughts returned to how Danny, when interviewed, had gone through the fall of wickets in proving that he must have been at the ground the whole time.

Ray was sure, however, that he had mentioned Bob Short being run out, when in actual fact he had been stumped. There was no way on this earth that Danny could have got it wrong, unless, just unless, he had read it from the scorebook.

The hairs started to tingle on the back of his neck as he suddenly realised the significance of the phone call to Allison. What if the reason Danny had spent ten minutes going through the scorebook was to learn what had happened in the match whilst he was somewhere else?

He decided to call everyone together for a meeting in the incident room at noon to explain the significance of what he had just learned.

Ray went through the logic of his thinking to everyone and the team did not need a lot of convincing that he was on the right track.

They decided to concentrate their whole effort on the movements of Danny from the time the match started to the point when it was abandoned.

At around 2.00 p.m. the breakthrough came, and it was through a brilliant piece of detective work from one of the younger officers.

Sean Williams had only been with the department for just under a year but he happened to notice that there was a difference between two photographs of Danny Maguire, one taken at the beginning of the match and the other just before tea-time.

Tapping on the door of his immediate boss Mike Salter, he was ushered in and invited to take a seat.

'Governor, as you may or not know, fast bowlers like to polish the cricket ball before they bowl it because it creates a swing movement to the ball as it approaches the batsman.

'This has always been done by vigorously shining the ball on the bowler's flannels just before he comes in to bowl. The more the ball is polished, the more it tends to swing and hence the more chance the batsman will be deceived.

'Nobody has ever worked out why shining one side of the ball causes it to move in the air but it has always been an important part of a fast bowler's armoury.

'Bowler's wives are known to hate this routine because the stain it leaves on the flannels or trousers is incredibly difficult to remove in the wash.'

Leaning forward Sean placed two photographs on Mike's desk and continued.

'This is a photo taken at the beginning of the match and you can plainly see that on the inside of his right thigh there is a long red stain that has not been totally removed by washing.

'Well now we come to the interesting bit, because if you look at this second photograph of Danny, taken later in the day just after teatime, you will see there are no stains on his trousers whatsoever.'

It took about a nanosecond for the penny to drop and as Mike looked up from his desk, they both said in unison, 'Which means, at some point he must have changed his trousers!'

Mike was ecstatic and couldn't wait to pull the team together to announce the news that they had a new suspect.

Later in the day, another vital piece of evidence came to light after investigating the video footage that had been filmed by one of the visitors. The footage had been taken in a panoramic sweep of the ground, firstly to the left and then brought all the way back to the starting place.

On the first sweep it was possible to see Danny just as he was approaching the entrance to the car park but on reversing the sweep, there was no sign of him whatsoever which meant that he must have entered the car park.

The significance of this was that his house was just a few minutes' walk from the rear of the cricket club's car park, but the most telling part was that the footage was taken just at 2.30 p.m. and within the murder timeframe suggested by the coroner.

Once again everyone was called into the incident room and this time it was Mike Salter that addressed the team.

'Folks through some fantastic investigative work it would appear that we have a new credible suspect. Firstly, we know that Danny Maguire disappeared into the car park at exactly 2.30 p.m.

He subsequently visited the scorebox at around 3.15 p.m. for about ten minutes and finally went into bat at about 3.45 p.m. We also now know that at some stage in the afternoon he changed his cricket flannels.

'I think he went home, murdered his wife and then went to the scorebox to learn what had happened in the match while he was away in order to establish his alibi.

'At some point he probably discovered some blood on his flannels and changed into a clean pair.

'Whether we have enough to charge him will depend on the Criminal Prosecution Service, but we certainly have enough to bring him back for further questioning.

'A lot will depend on his account of whether Bob Short was stumped or run out. We now know for certain that he was stumped but Sarah Miles had mistakenly entered in Bundary's scorebook that he had been run out.

'If he sticks to that story, we know one hundred per cent that he did not see what actually happened on the cricket pitch and that he had just read it from the scorebook.

'In any event we are just going to have to find the original pair of flannels that he was wearing. The only possible reason that he would have changed them is because they were blood-stained.

'He must have changed them at home before he returned to the cricket ground. He could have hidden them somewhere in the house or stuffed them inside his shirt and got rid of them nearby.

'We need a search warrant for his house and we also need to look in the hedgerows around the cricket ground and every inch of space in the pavilion and the surrounding areas.'

When Danny returned from work on the Monday evening there were three police cars and six officers waiting on his drive to greet him.

He was shown the warrant to search his home and under sufferance he unlocked the front door for the officers to enter, before being handcuffed and driven off for further questioning at Portishead.

By the time he arrived in Portishead, Danny was in a foul mood and kept asking on what grounds he had been arrested. He insisted that any interview would have to be conducted in the presence of the duty solicitor and he was held in the cells until one could be found.

By the time the duty officer arrived just before 8.00 p.m. Danny was spitting feathers.

He was taken into the interview room and once again introduced to the senior investigating officer, detective chief inspector Ray Stephens and also his senior crime investigating sergeant Sally Marshall.

Danny was read his Miranda rights but it was fairly obvious that he was going to waive his right to silence as he launched into a verbal tirade from the word go.

'Why on earth have you guys dragged me back here for further questioning when you should be out there trying to find my wife's killer?

'As if I have not gone through enough emotional trauma over the last few days, you are now going to subject me to even more stupid questions that will get you absolutely nowhere.'

Sally who was highly trained in interview technique tried to immediately calm things down by speaking in a quiet, almost apologetic, conciliatory tone.

'Look, Danny, it's pointless getting angry because we have a job to do and that includes asking some questions that we need answers to. The sooner we can clear things up the sooner we will be able to release you.'

It appeared to do the trick and Danny seemed to calm down and become more co-operative as Ray started with the well-prepared questions that were to take Danny down a very difficult path.

'OK, Danny, when you were first interviewed regarding your movements on the day of Helen's murder, it was made very clear to us that you were at the ground all afternoon and in fact you could recall the match details and also the fall of each wicket as it happened.

'Now, I would like to take you back to when the score was 120 for the loss of 4 wickets and Bob Short had just reached

50 runs, which we all know is somewhat of a milestone for a batsman. Could you please just talk us through his dismissal?'

Without hesitation Danny answered immediately, 'Well yes, it's just at that point when he was run out going for a quick single, which was never really on the cards. Someone is run out when they don't make it to the opposite end of the pitch before the bails are removed. He ran as hard as he could but he just couldn't get his bat down in time.'

'Yes, yes, I understand that,' Ray replied. 'But the problem is, Danny, that is not what happened and I wonder if you would like to change anything you have told us.'

Danny began to look a little nervous.

'Well, it's in the scorebook as a run out and that's how I remember it, so what's the big deal?'

Ray wasted no time in replying and leaning forward spoke deliberately slowly.

'Well, it's in your scorebook as a run out but that is not what happened Danny and as you said you were watching the match, so would you like to re-consider exactly how Bob Short was out?'

There was no way Ray was going to tell Danny that Bob Short had accidentally fallen over and was subsequently stumped by the wicket-keeper and he wanted to give him enough rope to hang himself.

Danny decided to go on the offensive.

'What's all this rubbish about how Bob Short was out got to do with the murder of my wife, have you lot completely lost the plot or what?'

Sally, with her calming tone, decided to intervene again.

'Danny, we are just trying to establish your movements on the afternoon of the cricket match because we also have it on video that at 2.30 p.m. you were walking around the cricket ground but suddenly disappeared into the car park.

'We know that from there it is just a short walk through the field back to your house. The next time there is any sighting of you is when you popped into the scorebox to have a word with your scorer Sarah Miles at about 3.15 p.m. It's quite interesting that you spent about ten minutes looking at the scorebook before moving on.'

As a well-rehearsed double act, as Sally paused for breath, Ray moved in.

'Danny, there is one more thing that we would like to run past you. Like all good fast bowlers, you like to shine the ball on your trousers to keep the swing going for as long as possible.

'We all know that the wives hate it because the stain is incredibly difficult to remove with washing and there is inevitably a residual stain.

'Now this is a photograph taken of you walking out to the wicket with Jack Reed, the Fieldhouses captain just before the start of play.

'You can clearly see that there is quite a large stain on the inside of your right thigh, do you agree?'

Ray pushed the photo forwards for Danny to see it who nodded his agreement.

'Well now, this is another photograph taken just before tea and abracadabra the stain has gone.

'How do you think that happened, Danny?'

Danny suddenly went a whiter shade of pale, threw his arms up in the air and replied very calmly.

'I have absolutely no idea, what you are talking about and why it has any relevance to anything.'

Ray decided it was time to stop playing cat and mouse and moved in for the kill.

'Well, I will tell you what relevance I think it has because I think you have been telling us a pack of porkies. I think what happened that afternoon is that when your team was batting you knew you had enough time to go home, murder your wife and then return to the ground. As you were the last man in to bat, you had a window of opportunity to last an hour before you would be needed. Your idea of going to the scorebox and reading what had happened in the match whilst you were away from the ground was brilliant.

'You thought it would give you a cast iron alibi, which of course, it should have done.

'Except, Danny, you had an inexperienced scorer in Sarah Miles who happened to enter the wrong reason for the dismissal of Bob Short.

'Bob Short was stumped, not run out, and if you had seen the dismissal with your own eyes there is no way you would have got it wrong.

'I think in stabbing Helen, you inevitably got some blood on your white cricket trousers and had to change before returning to the ground in a spare pair you took from the wardrobe.

'I think you have been spinning us a lie and this murder was coldly calculated from the word go.

'I am convinced that Helen had told you she was pregnant with Oliver Traves' baby and that they were running away together.

'It was just too much for you to bear and you planned the whole thing using your presence at the cricket ground as your cast-iron alibi. Have I got it right, Danny?'

Danny looked blankly into space and spoke two words, 'No Comment.'

The duty solicitor thought it was a good time to bring a halt to proceedings and Danny was remanded in custody overnight, awaiting further questioning the following morning. He cut a very forlorn figure as he was led away to his cell.

Mike Salter had been hanging around the office, desperate to hear how the interview had gone with Ray and Sally. The three of them sat down to consider the situation.

There was no good news from the search of the house to find the missing cricket flannels and Ray was starting to get desperate.

'We have to find those trousers because everything we have is just circumstantial. The criminal prosecution service wouldn't even take it to court unless we have some evidence that definitely links Danny to the murder.

'The scorebook and car park evidence only has merit if we can link it to the blood-stained flannels. We just have to find them or I am afraid he walks free.'

Time was moving on and Mike suggested phoning a few of the team to meet early the following morning at the cricket ground for a thorough search of the club and the surrounding areas.

Half a dozen officers agreed to meet at 7.00 a.m. and Mike said he would tag along as he still had a key to the pavilion. As there was little else that could be achieved by hanging round the office, it was time to call it a day and get some sleep.

It showed great team spirit that when Mike pulled onto the Bundary cricket ground car park the following day at exactly 7.00 am, all six officers had already arrived.

The pavilion was searched whilst another team trawled through the undergrowth surrounding the ground but there was nothing to be found other than empty cans and the occasional beer bottle.

The last place to be searched was the area around the scorebox. As it was an old wooden structure, rabbits had burrowed underneath leaving a few significant scrapes but there was also a much larger hole that looked like an old badger den.

Stretching deep inside Mike suddenly felt something soft that was definitely not a badger. Pulling at the fabric, he nearly fainted as out came a pair of dirty cricket flannels, covered in spots of blood.

There was a whooping and a hollering from the team that would have graced any cup final goal. To their absolute delight they had found the smoking gun.

Ray Stephens was very much a man of habit and always left his house at precisely 8.15 a.m. every morning. He was just picking up his car keys from the hall table when the phone rang.

It was a moment he would never forget for the rest of his life. An ecstatic Mike Salter relayed the news to him that the smoking gun had indeed been found and Ray couldn't wait to get into the office and congratulate everyone.

Back at Portishead there was an anxious ten minutes whilst the stains on the cricket flannels were compared to the stains on the photo taken of Danny just before the match started.

By blowing up the size of the photo to the size of the exact stains on the pair of flannels, it was obvious for all to see that they were identical, apart from the spots of blood that were evident at irregular intervals.

Danny was brought from the holding cell to the interview room where he was once again joined by the duty solicitor, Ray Stephens and Sally Marshall.

Ray wasted no time in presenting the plastic bag containing the cricket flannels that had been found that morning and as the blood appeared to drain from Danny's face, he slumped down into one of the chairs.

Ray was in no mood to entertain any pleasantries and after all the formalities of interview protocol had been completed, he wasted little time in setting out the scene.

'Danny, let's try and make this interview as short as possible because we now have all the evidence, we need to charge you with the murder of your wife Helen on the afternoon of Saturday 30th March at your home No. 23 Winslow Gardens Bundary.

'For the sake of completeness, we have a video of you walking around the cricket ground but then disappearing into the car park at exactly 2.30 p.m.

'We then have you appearing in the scorebox at around 3.15 p.m. when you spent about ten minutes getting up to speed on what happened in the match but your inexperienced scorer Sarah Miles had unfortunately entered the stumping of Bob Short incorrectly in your scorebook as a run out.

'You have played cricket for most of your life and there is no way you would mix up a stumping with a run out which only goes to prove that you were not at the ground, as you insist you were, to see what actually happened.

'We then have a photograph of you going into tea wearing a different pair of flannels to which you started the match and these are the relevant photographs. One picture shows the heavy red ball staining on the inside of the thigh and lo and behold the other picture shows no staining whatsoever.

'Finally, Danny, we have one soiled pair of cricket trousers, retrieved this morning, from underneath the scorebox with the staining on the inside of the thigh matching perfectly the staining in the photograph of you just before play began.

'Oh, and the cricket flannels have blood splattered all over them which I have absolutely no doubt will be a match for Helen's blood when we have them analysed.

'Or would you like to save us the trouble, Danny, and tell us that the blood will definitely be a match because you were the man who committed the murder?'

In the slight pause that followed, Sally took the opportunity to move in with a sledgehammer blow.

'Look, Danny, before you answer, we would like you to consider a few facts. We have motive for the crime in that Helen was pregnant with another man's baby, which must have been devastating for you knowing that you were infertile. In addition to that they planned to run away together and start a new life.

'We have opportunity in that your home was only a short walk from the cricket ground and the murder was committed at a time that your team was not fielding.

'Finally, we have an abundance of evidence that both ties you to the scene of the crime and more importantly your attempt to dispose of a pair of blood-stained cricket flannels which we can prove you were wearing.

'So, we have motive, opportunity and evidence that I think in your sporting parlance would be described as game set and match.

'Any court in the land would relish the prospect of trying this case as a very well-conceived pre-meditated murder that carries a very lengthy prison sentence. If, however, you admit the crime and save the judicial system an enormous amount of time and money, the judge is far more likely to be lenient when awarding the sentence.'

Danny looked a defeated man and after a few words with the duty solicitor, he finally gave in.

'Okay, okay, I admit that I was holding the knife that killed Helen, but what happened is not at all how the whole thing unfolded.

'A few days before the match, I happened to overhear Helen arranging to meet this Oliver Traves guy at our house around lunchtime because she knew I would be at the cricket ground for most of the day.

'I had heard rumours that she was having an affair with someone from the "Wet Whistle" who was a small-time low life drug dealer but also a nasty piece of work and I decided that it was a good opportunity to catch them together and have it out with this guy, once and for all.

'When I walked into the kitchen they were chatting away and it soon got very nasty. After a few minutes of arguing Helen announced that she was pregnant with his child and that they planned to run away together.

'It was at that point that I completely lost it and took the biggest knife I could find from the kitchen drawer and went for Oliver Traves.

'It all happened in a few seconds because as I lunged forward, Helen instinctively tried to shield him by standing in the way and the only protection she had was a flimsy summer dress. It was too late to pull back and the knife.'

At this point Danny completely broke down and sobbed like a child with his bowed head held in both hands.

In a moment of motherly understanding Sally wanted to tell Danny that Oliver Traves had met his comeuppance in Dubrovnik but realised that nothing she could say was going to make him feel any better.

He was allowed a few moments to pull himself together and was then taken to the duty sergeant and formerly charged with the murder of Helen Maguire.

When Ray and Sally returned to the incident room, Mike Salter and a few of the investigative team were anxious to hear whether Danny had confessed to the crime.

Ray explained to the team that Danny had admitted to the stabbing of Helen as an accident but not to the murder as a pre-meditated act.

He went on to say that it would be up to the crime prosecution service to decide whether it was a well-planned murder or manslaughter with the crime committed in a moment of anger.

In any event their job had been done and he thanked everyone for their hard work and time that had been put into a very complicated case.

When all the paperwork had been completed Ray and Mike decided to call it a day and head for a well-earned pint at the local pub.

They were both in a reflective mood as Mike sat down and started the conversation.

'Do you think it was an accident, Guv, or do you think he had planned it all along knowing that his alibi would be hard to break down?'

Ray thought long and hard before answering, 'I would like to think it was an accident but to have the presence of mind to go to the scorebox and construct an alibi from the details of the scorebook, takes some doing when you have supposedly just stabbed your wife to death by accident.

'Presumably, Oliver Traves fled for his life after the murder and that's why the five grand was left in the drier because Danny knew nothing about the blackmailing of Paul Mason. I also suspect that Oliver Traves left the country in a hurry because he thought Danny would be seeking him out to get his revenge.

'It will be fascinating to see how the CPS does proceed and whether they go after Danny for murder or manslaughter.

'For sure it has been the strangest case I've ever worked on.

'A drug-dealing cricketer from Wolverhampton finds the murdered body of a young woman and ten days later becomes a hero as an undercover agent helping to smash a ten-million-pound narcotics smuggling ring in the Balkans.

'On top of that another cricketer becomes the prime suspect in the murder case simply because a young girl enters the wrong details of how a wicket fell in her scorebook.

'Well, Mike, you just couldn't write it.'

THE END